Sin on a Burning Heart

SINS
BOOK THREE

RHIANNON FUTCH

Contents

One

Jasmine

We haven't seen the house since we hired the decorator. Chloe, Scarlett, and I spent a lot of time talking about what we wanted our place to look like when we finally got to live in it again. A dark gothic style is what we settled on, and then finding a designer was another chore.

Once we did, we gave her free rein so long as it remained dark gothic with our color choices.

Tonight is the night, we got the call to come home to see what masterpiece she has wrought. As I drive over I can't help but scan the cars and people walking. Everyone says that Mikael must be dead but I can't shake the feeling that he is still alive somewhere, just waiting for the right moment to pounce.

That feeling is why I have been training so hard and working long days at my magic. Hekate has been teaching me things that Helen would find abhorrent. Offensive spells that will help me keep my family safe. Helen is teaching me control and balance, both of which make it much easier to understand and use the magics that Hekate teaches me.

Pulling into the driveway I am stunned. The relatively big house we bought has been replaced with a massive creation of Leonidas's design, but it was unfinished when we saw it last. The outside had not been finished because Leonidas had said he wanted to make it a surprise. It is gorgeous. I get out of the car to get a better look and I am loving what I see. The shutters are a deep red and the house itself is black. The roof is a red to match the shutters, and looking closer I see the shutters are functional!

The door matches, and the porch extending the length of the front of the house has plants and chairs with hella cushions, little tables perfect for coffee and a book. I could live on the porch, but I am dying to see the inside.

Chloe calls out from the porch, "Girl! Would you come on? We want to see the inside!"

I hurry to join them, Chloe opens the door slowly so we can take it in. My jaw drops. The entry is massive and open. The floor is tiled with something that looks like marble, white with veins of black and grey running through it. I am sure the designer will tell us all about it in her final write up. A gorgeous staircase is off to the right, a black runner padding the stairs.

We walk through the first floor, each room is gorgeous and dark. It gives gothic vibes all the way around. We are fully delighted and head up the stairs to find our bedrooms. We each chose a room and at the top of the stairs we split up to each go see our room. Mine is at the far end of the hall. I pause for a moment in front of the door, opening it slowly so I can take it all in before I step foot in the room. It is magnificent. A giant bed dominates the room, canopied and curtained. The curtains are black, and as I step closer I see there are two sets of curtains. One is a sheer black with lace accents and the other is a heavy type I could use to shut out the sunlight if I needed to. The walls of my room are a deep red and there are gold accents in various places, just enough to break up the red and black of the room without being gaudy or overpowering. The furniture is dark and simple, which I love. I have a fireplace! It is surrounded by some black tile stuff and it looks ready to go. I walk over to inspect it better and see that it is a gas fireplace, so I won't need to worry about collecting wood. Fireplace inspected, now I need to check out my bed. The duvet is black and gold, the material is silky on the top and soft as down on the bottom. Pulling back the bedding and kicking off my shoes, I climb into the bed, it is glorious. I didn't know that beds could feel this good.

I want to stay here in this spot forever. As I lay in my bed enjoying the comfort my mind drifts back to the problem I seem to spend all my time obsessing over. Mikael. I know he is out there somewhere. But where? Even some of Leonidas's sketchier contacts came up dry. Where the hell could he be hiding? Or maybe I should accept what everyone else thinks. Maybe he is dead and I am just not accepting the fact that he is gone. I just, something in my gut says he isn't gone. It's the same thing that always told me when I was about to walk into Fabio's fist again that antsy, anxious feeling of something bad coming for me.

That feeling has never been wrong before. I know everyone wants me to let this go and accept that he is dead, but I think I need to trust my instincts. And Hekate has not said he is dead! That's right! When I told her that everyone thinks he is dead but I feel like he isn't she said I should always trust my feelings, they wouldn't lead me astray.

I hear footsteps coming down the hall and I look to the door to see Chloe and Scarlet. "This bed is amazing. You two should come try it. The duvet! Silky on one side, soft and warm on the other."

They crawl into the bed with me and we all snuggle up under the covers to talk about our love of the house and everything in it.

Two

Jasmine

It's lessons with Helen day again. I love learning from her. She is grounding me in the basics and teaching me a control that I don't think I could have achieved without her. Some of the things she had me doing I thought for sure were absolute garbage. All the meditation and centering and grounding and working on little magics over and over till I thought my head would explode. But now I can do those things with ease and it has translated into an easier time grasping the lessons that Hekate has given me.

So while Helen has been teaching me to work with the elements and keep them in check while I do so, Hekate has taught me how to fuck shit up. Hekate taught me about creating a tornado. We kept it small, but I can definitely destroy some things with one. The only issue with that, and with a lot of other elemental magic, is bystanders. I am not trying to send random people off to meet their end by accident. If I end someone, I want it to be intentional.

Pulling into a space at the book store I put the car in park. I sit there for a minute as this weird itchy feeling moves through me. I feel itchy in my bones and it is all I can do not to try and scratch my way into them to ease the itch. I finally get out as the itch eases but I have to ask Helen about this, maybe she knows something about this. Or at least how to make it stop?

Walking into the store I wave at the person working the register tonight. They nod as I keep walking. I breathe deeply, the scent particular to book stores is something I have always loved. Now that I have money and time, my book collection is growing. Walking through a book store on a regular basis is probably helping that right along.

The hallway at the back of the store is quiet as usual. I see Helen bustling about at the table where we do most of our lessons. Looks like I will be playing with all the elements tonight. She is setting out dishes of earth, water, one of twigs, and a container of smoke. Her idea of using smoke so that we could see what I was doing with the air is the best. She can see exactly what I have the air doing and so can I.

She sees me and says, "Jasmine! Hello! Come, sit. I have everything set up, we are going to have some fun tonight. We are also going to talk about the prophecy and that won't be as much fun but it is necessary."

"Before we get started, can I ask you something?"

"Of course, I'll answer as best I can."

"My bones keep itching. This is a new thing and it isn't all the time. But when it does happen it has me wanting to scratch all the way to the source. Have you ever heard of something like that happening? I don't think it is likely to mean I am sick, because well, vampire."

Helen paces, one hand on her chin and the other on her elbow, "I haven't heard of that specific symptom but I have heard of omens and foretellings and such manifesting as physical symptoms. It is very possible that it is a warning of some sort. What was happening around you when this manifested?"

"It happened just now when I was getting here. My bones lit up. I sat in the car for a little bit till I could move without wanting to do damage to myself."

"Is this the only time it has happened?"

"No. There were other times, but they were so fleeting I chalked it up as a weird hunger pang."

She stops pacing and faces me, "I can't say for certain what this means, but my gut tells me it is a warning. You will need to be mindful and aware of other signs. Chances are, other signs were sent but when you didn't see them or hear them or understand them to be signs, Spirit got louder. More insistent. So, my best advice is to pay attention to things around you. Not everything is a sign and sometimes it is hard to tell what is. Ask for clarity. Out loud. Let Spirit know that you are listening, and what kind of message will help you understand the best. What you will be watching for. And the most important part to all this, watch for those things. Because if Spirit wants you to have a message, it will get louder until you get the message or the thing happens. It is usually better to listen to Spirit."

"Isn't Spirit just the Gods talking to us?"

"No. Spirit is something bigger than the Gods. Something other. From what my deities have told me recently, Spirit also sends them signs. If they don't pay attention the signs get really loud I am told."

"Oh. Ok. I guess that answers my question. Thank you."

She claps her hands together in front of her, "Now, how about a lesson to distract us from annoying things we don't yet understand?"

Two hours later my lessons are done for the night. I have browsed the book store and picked up some smutty romance to take home with me. Walking out to my car with keys in hand I see something coming at me out of the corner of my eye right as my bones light up with that terrible itch, I drop my purchases as I spin to face the threat. Of nothing. Nothing whatsoever is there and I just dropped my books for nothing.

Great.

I pick up the books and dust them off, all the while my bones are on fire. I don't know what the reason is for this, but it sure does suck. I still feel like something is here, like I should be braced for an attack. But my magic says there is nothing and my other senses agree. I check my backseat and get in the car, locking the doors before I start it. The itching in my bones is fading now. I don't know what the hell is up with this.

As I leave the parking lot I start talking to Spirit while I drive. "I want to hear you, but this bone itching thing, I don't understand it. If it is meant to warn me of danger, I need a different sign. Can we do something like um… a whisper? Can you whisper to me? I would really like a clear and audible whisper. If that isn't possible, maybe something like a ladybug or a butterfly landing on my hand?" I wait for a response but nothing happens as I continue my drive home. Who knows? Maybe Spirit wasn't even listening.

Three

Mikael

My office in this house has never been a favorite. Perhaps I will have Vigo choose another room and it set up as my office. He seems to have an instinct for exactly what I will find pleasurable in so many ways. I am still considering the many ways he pleasures me when he walks in with a tray saying, "Here you go sir, got to keep your strength up. You're all healed up but you need to be extra when you face her."

As he pours a glass of fresh blood for me I tell him, "Ah Vigo, I don't plan to face her at her just full strength. If I face her at all. I have someone coming to work for me that should turn the tables nicely."

He brings me the glass and handing it over asks, "Who exactly is going to do this for you?"

"Is that jealousy I hear Vigo? Shame on you. Jealousy is beneath you." I hear a knocking at the door, "That must be him. Show him in Vigo. Best behavior or I won't punish you tonight."

His shoulders drop briefly, "If you insist."

He returns quickly with the man that has come to see me. "Hake, welcome to my home. Please, sit, and we will get straight to business."

Hake seats himself across from me and Vigo excuses himself to go tend our laundry. Hake raises a brow at Vigo's possessiveness and I shrug. "Hake, you know what I want. Jasmine has to either be my property or eliminated. I know you are capable of doing the job, but you have insisted that we speak of your payment only in person. What exactly is it that you want?"

Hake's lips lift in a slow smile, "I want to be one of you. I have power but my lifetime is fleeting. I want to stick around. My proposal is this, I help you to achieve your ends and then you turn me. Make me a vampire like yourself."

I laugh, long and loud. This is so perfect. "That is all you want? Just to be turned? No money, favors, or anything else?"

"That is the price for my help. I can acquire money and favors on my own. None of that will help me live forever. And the Philosopher's Stone doesn't appear to do what the histories have hinted at so it is useless. Now, will you agree to my price?"

"I agree. Once Jasmine is either my property or dead, I will turn you."

"Excellent. What information do you have on her?"

"She is beautiful. This incarnation has been especially good to her. Blond hair, blue eyes, great rack and an ass you could bounce a quarter off of. Her attitude is shit, entirely too enamored of herself and thinks she is far above her station in life. She has a powerful magic but no training. I turned her in to the council and her fear of the council should continue to keep her from seeking any training. Her magic does seek to defend her though. And that can be dangerous. I assume you have ways of nullifying untrained magic. She is one of three that I have sired, and therefore quite strong. Do not allow her to engage with you physically, she will kill you. She has killed numerous vampires older than her." I pause for a sip of the blood in my glass, "Her beauty though, that will draw you in. Beware. She is as deadly as she is beautiful. I also have her address," I pick up the paper I have it written on from the table beside me and hand it over to him, "and it is an easy enough place to find."

Hake nods, "I will go watch her for a few days before I decide what my—our next move will be."

"Perfect. I will call Vigo to show you out." Vigo enters just then and I raise an eyebrow because he was obviously listening at the door. He asks Hake to please follow him and they both leave my office. I lean back in my chair to enjoy the rest of this glass.

Four

Jasmine

Scarlett and I sat down three hours ago to watch a movie and we enjoyed the time together so much that we just kept watching movies. We are just starting movie four when there is a knock at the door. Scarlett offers to get it while I get the movie we picked pulled up.

I hear footsteps coming back and I look up to find Leonidas walking in, Scarlett is no where to be found. "What happened to Scarlett?"

He tells me, "She said she had monopolized your time for the past few hours and she wanted to let me have time with you too."

I am continually amazed at the way my friends are able to be so giving with me and each other. I have never had people in my life that were this good to me. I take a breath and chase away the misty eyes threatening happy tears, "She is too sweet. Are you here to watch movies with me or do you want to talk or fool around? What shall we do?"

His face scrunches as he tries to decide, "Can we do more than one?"

"I'm game."

"Ok, then I have news first. My loan is nearly paid off and everyone is making a ridiculous amount of money on this venture. I have two more houses to get sold and even with reinvesting I won't need to get another loan to float this." He is pacing the room in front of the tv as he talks and he is so animated. His joy and excitement make me so happy for him. "I will be putting the vast majority of my share into it as investment capital, but this will be the last time. I have two houses that just went on the market, and two more are nearly ready. We still have fifteen more sites to go through!"

Clapping my hands together I exclaim, "Leonidas, that's excellent! I am so happy for you! You and your clan are really pulling together and thriving!" I jump up and run over to hug him, he catches me up in his arms and spins me around as he holds me close. As he sets me down my bones start itching like crazy and I see something dark coming at us out of the corner of my eye, I spin around ready to attack it and there is nothing.

I straighten and Leonidas clears his throat, "Um. Jasmine, what was that?"

I fold my arms across my body, "I thought I saw something coming at us."

He pulls me into his arms, and I love the feel of being there but I can't shake the feeling that something was here. He asks, "Are you ok? Has something been going on that I don't know about to have you this jumpy in your own house?"

"I—I just feel like something is coming. I have this weird itch in my bones that only shows up sometimes and this isn't the first time I have seen something coming at me but there didn't seem to be anything there." I walk over to gaze out the window, "And I feel like Mikael is still alive. Like he is coming for me."

Leonidas moves to my side and puts an arm around me, "Damn. I didn't know. I'm sorry. I still feel like Mikael is probably dead. But, I trust your instincts. So maybe he is alive. How about we go visit my mom? She is— she's fading. Sometimes what she says is really disjointed. She seems to be half here and half there. I don't know why she is hanging on. But her predictions are more horrifying in their accuracy lately. She might be able to tell you. And she did like seeing you."

"Really?"

"Yeah. She said it made her happy to see you arriving, that it gave her hope."

"I would like that. When can we go?"

"Now if you want."

"Let me grab shoes and my bag."

The nursing home is unchanged. It is like a small oasis in time for the residents. Unchanging and nicer than most of the ones I have seen. But I suppose the difference between the neighborhoods is bigger than I want to think about. We walk through the quiet halls, they smell of cinnamon and allspice. I wonder if they feed the residents cookies on a regular basis or they just scent the air with those things?

He knocks on the door to his mother's room as he opens it. She is sitting up in her bed and she turns her head to look at us. Her eyes are completely white and her hair is sticking out in tufts, it is the creepiest thing I have ever seen. Then she says, "I have been waiting for you," as she brings a hand up to point at me. It is all I can do not to turn and run.

"Hello Ms. Manoie, it has been some time since I saw you last. I hear you aren't doing so great."

She barks a laugh, "I am nearly dead. Of course I am not doing so great. It's fine now. I was waiting for you. We knew you would come."

I look around the room to see if someone is waiting to pounce on me, because my nerves are shot right now with this level of creep show. "Um, who is we?"

"Spirit and I. We knew. We saw. We saw you breaking the prophecy. Your actions, we couldn't have predicted them back then, they were unthinkable. You changed things, the prophecy swings between possibilities now." Her voice changes, it sounds like someone else is in there with her, "The path forward depends on your choices. If you choose the devil of the light all will be lost. You must stay alive and unclaimed by him. His evil hides in the light while pointing fingers and the ones in the dark. He will try to ruin you. To break you." She starts to glow and her voice gets deeper, *"DO NOT LET THAT ONE CLAIM YOU."* The glow fades and her voice goes back to being her own, "The way forward is following your heart. Keep your heart open to love or risk becoming that which seeks to destroy you." She turns to Leonidas, "Come here sweet boy, give your mother one last hug before I go." He walks into her arms and I hear her whisper, "You are so loved. I will miss your face most of all dear boy. Be well and take care of her, she will need your love almost as much as the world needs her."

Tears flow down my face as her arms fall away from Leonidas, her eyes closed for the last time. Wiping away the blood tears, I leave the room and walk to the nurse's station to let them know she has passed and Leonidas is saying his goodbyes. One of the nurses says, "So it was you she was waiting for. She sat up this afternoon and she looked at the doorway every time one of us came to check on her but then she would look away and seem disappointed when she saw us. She refused dinner, said she was waiting and dinner wouldn't matter soon. That kind of thing never fails to give us the shivers."

I nod and turn to walk back down the hall as they start making calls. All I can think about is her last words to me. Did she really mean what it sounded like? Keep my heart open or become Mikael? Is that really what happened to him? Did he close his heart off and turn into the monster he is now? What happens if one of my lovers decides to break things off? What if my heart gets broken again? Am I one heartbreak away from fucking the entire world over? How can I prevent this? Can I just not fall in love? Is that an answer or will that bring it along just the same? She told him that I would need his love? Can I really rely on Leonidas to not break my heart? Or is the world doomed because the Gods chose wrong?

Leonidas walks out of the room and the attendants waiting walk in. A doctor and nurse stay to speak with him. He looks like he is holding on by a thread, I walk over to him and slip my arm around his waist. He loops an arm around my shoulders and holds on tight as he finishes speaking with them. They enter the room as we turn to leave. The hallway seems never ending as I feel him straining to walk at a human pace with every step he takes. We make it outside and he draws in a deep breath, finally letting the tears slide down his face with a sob.

The parking lot is quiet as we walk to the truck, each immersed in our own thoughts. My bones flare with a burn and I stop short when Mikael appears in front of me, Leonidas hits him with a quick jab but all that happens is smoke flows around his hand and reforms. Mikael laughs as he fades away. When nothing more happens we continue on to the truck. Leonidas says, "Can you drive?"

"Of course. Just to ease my mind, you saw that, right?"

He nods, "I did. And I saw it fade away to nothing. I don't know what is going on, but you were not alone in seeing that."

"Ok. I need to talk to Helen about this."

"I agree. I am glad I didn't put my whole body into that swing. Um, I know this isn't a great time but can I ask you a favor?"

"Yes! What can I do for you?"

"My mom's funeral will be in a few days. It has been set up forever, she just never told me the date. It is set to be in the late afternoon to early evening. Would you go with me? I really would like you to be there, especially since you are the only reason I can go."

"I would be honored."

Five

Jasmine

"Helen, I need to talk to you before we start tonight."

"What's on your mind Jasmine?"

I wait as she seats herself across from me, "Remember the bones thing I told you about?"

"I do. Have you learned anything new about it?"

"I think I have. Last night I was walking out of the nursing home and Mikael appeared in front of me. He looked solid and Leonidas threw a punch at him only he was smoke and just laughed as he reformed. Then he faded away. Still laughing. I have been asking that the itching bones thing not be how I am alerted to whatever the problem is and this time it was a brief flare right before he appeared."

"Oh my. Well, we knew he would be coming back. My best guess is that the itching, the flare, those are definitely warning signs; and it is highly probable that they are related to Mikael acting against you. Now that you know that, we can try to figure out how to make it work for you. As for the shade. Well, that is more of a problem. You need a powerful witch to do that. I know that Mikael has very little left after what was meant to be yours went to you. So who did he hire?"

"That isn't even the worst part. We were at the nursing home to see Leonidas's mom. She is— was, a powerful psychic. She saw visions of the future. And what she told me... she told me that the prophecy is broken and that I must not let the demon of the light claim me. Also to keep my heart open or risk becoming um... how did she put it? Oh, that which seeks to destroy me."

Hekate appears in the chair next to me, "Her vision is correct. You have broken the prophecy. It is mostly just garbage on fancy paper now. Unless things snap back into place. That isn't likely to happen though. The reason for this is that it was supposed to hinge on you being with one person that would be your partner and the two of you would seek to be better. Only you didn't want to be tied to just one and so now you have three. All of whom are decent people that will seek to do better by the planet, though most would consider them to be bad people for being vampires and for the amount of murders they commit. It wouldn't matter to them that they are ridding the world of rapists and killers. They are more concerned with the appearance of things. Tiresome really."

I shrug, "People are like that. Things just need to be pretty on the outside, the inside doesn't matter."

Hekate and Helen nod, Hekate continues, "No one is very sure what would need to be done to put the prophecy back on course or if that would even be the best plan. You just do what the nice lady said and let your heart guide you. You, my best acolyte from so long ago, will do just fine. I knew you would be the right choice for this, especially since Mikael was already signed up for the other side. I am so proud of you Jasmine."

I can't help but be very concerned about all of this. I broke the prophecy? "Are we sure that I am the right one for all this? I mean. I have been a whole fuck up this entire life so far. I was a fuck up in a lot of the other ones too. Are we really sure that I am the right one for the job? I feel like choices were made that are going to be regretted. Later. Soon. Very soon."

Hekate and Helen sigh, share a look, and Hekate says, "You continually look to protect those you care about and you even try to protect strangers. That is exactly what the world needs more of. I have faith in you. Just keep being you and working at finding your way. You are going to do great things."

Hekate disappears as soon as she finishes speaking. Helen has her hands clasped in front of her mouth, "Jasmine, I think she had a tear in her eye. She must really care for you. And I am just going to say, I know you can do this. Now, let's get to the lesson. I think today we are going to work on shielding. Barriers and protection. It would seem you are going to need those very soon."

A few hours later I have practiced shielding things until I can't even call my magic any more before Helen calls it a night. Even then she is telling me that I need to practice this at home, I need to get my home properly protected so that strange things can't just wander in. I laugh and tell her, "My roommates are not going to like it if I prevent them from coming in the house."

She scowls at me, "Go home young lady. And think about what I said. You need to get your house protected as soon as possible. If not for yourself then for your friends."

"I will, I promise I will work on it. I just have to figure out how to do it right for our circumstances. Thank you Helen, see you soon."

I walk through the book store slowly, savoring the sights and smells after our long training session. My body seems unaffected by all the practice, aside from my being hungry, but my mind is tired. I step out into the night air and take a deep breath, the briskness of autumn is in the air. I love it. The leaves falling remind me that all things change and change is a good thing.

I snap back to reality when my bones flare with a feeling like fire. Continuing toward the car as I scan and see Mikael appear in front of me, just a few feet away. My eyes narrow and he smiles, "Glad to see you ditched the loser."

Crossing my arms in front of me I say, "I see you learned a lesson about not appearing within reach. Why are you hear Mikael?"

He snarls at me, "Always with the mouth!" He stalks toward me and gets right in my face, "I can't wait to break you."

I swing my hands out and up to clap them together in the space his head is occupying, "I can't wait to show you again that it isn't happening. Walk away Mikael. I don't want to kill you."

He laughs as he fades away, "As if you could."

The house is bright when I get home and I am glad for it. I don't want to be alone after seeing Mikael again. Getting out of the car I run up the drive and get myself into the house. My magic is available again and I throw a shield around the house, this one just against magic. It won't do any good if Mikael shows up here at the house but it will keep him from sending any weird shades of himself at me.

I don't see anyone downstairs so I head for the kitchen to grab a couple bags of blood. Bags in hand I bite into one as I wander upstairs, listening for my room mates. I finally hear them in the laundry room. I walk up and lean against the door frame, just watching as they transfer laundry from one machine to another. Really, having multiple units in our house was the best and most bougie idea ever. Chloe sees me there and asks, "Why don't you join us in laundry day? I know you have laundry you need done."

"Of course I do. But I prefer to let it become all it can be before I take it down."

Scarlett snorts, "Meaning she is waiting till she has nothing to wear before she does laundry. Helen work you hard tonight?"

"She did. I thought I would die. But that isn't even the biggest event of the evening."

Chloe stops folding and turns to face me, "What happened?"

"Mikael appeared in front of me. Told me he was glad to see I ditched the loser and that he couldn't wait to break me."

Scarlett is the first to react, "First, what the fuck? Leonidas may not be everyone's cuppa but he is no loser. Second, the last time he tried you brought his house down around his head. I don't think he has thought this through."

I laugh, "Well, he isn't really known for that. At least not in regards to me. His actions have been erratic the entire time. Right now, I do at least have an answer to what is up with my bones. It is like a warning about him. Not a very good one because it makes me wild with itching and wanting to dig it out of my bones and it usually happens only seconds before something with him, but it is a warning. I guess it is something…"

Chloe has been deep in thought the whole time, "When you say appeared what exactly do you mean?"

"I mean he looked solid enough but he just appeared and then vanished in front of me. It happened with Leonidas too, but he appeared within reach when I was with Leonidas and had to wait to talk after his face reformed." I say with a chuckle at the memory. "And, I have a funeral to go to soon. Leonidas's mother died last night after giving me the spookiest damn predictions I have ever heard. Her eyes were all white. And I don't think it was all her. Then she died. The whole thing was sad and frightening at the same time."

"Oh shit," Chloe says, "tell Leonidas he has our sympathies. Is it a night funeral?"

"No. And that is part of why he wanted me to go. He said the only reason he can go is because of me."

Scarlett nods, "I get that. When my momma passed, I had to hide in a crypt near where she would be buried so I could feel like a part of it and then I spent some time at her grave after dark. I'm glad he is getting to say good-bye like this."

Chloe wraps her arms around herself, "I never knew where my mother was buried. One of the people from my village saw me and they knew I was supposed to be dead. They accused my mother of making a pact with a demon and they killed her. When I went to visit her in secret I found out what they had done."

"Oh Chloe," I say as I cross the room to hug her, "I am so sorry. What happened when you got there? How did you find out?"

I step back a little so she can speak and she says, "My mother's hut had been burnt to the ground when I arrived. She was one of the few survivors from before, but the ground under her hut was saturated with her blood. Her hut was away from the village, she didn't want to associate with any of them. She said her life was better alone. I had been bringing her supplies for some years. Making sure she had books and paper and plenty of food. When I found her home burnt to the ground and the ground soaked with her blood I was overcome with rage. I tracked the ones that murdered my mother back to our home village. I found the ring leader and I tortured him as he told me what they had done to her. They thought that I was an evil spirit and that I was attached to her. By killing her they would send me back to hell. They even had a ritual given to them by the holy man of our village. It was only the men of the village. The women, they had no idea. So I took every man that was part of the hunt for my mother and I hung him in the square. I made everyone come watch as I stabbed an artery in each with my hair stick. They bled out on the ground as I cursed the village. When they were dead I burned them where they hung and I made everyone stay to watch. The smell of burning flesh hung over the village for weeks after. When it was done, when there was nothing but some charred bits of bone left, I told the village to create a memorial to my mother right there, so they would never forget the demon that cursed that place.

I watched from the shadows for the next year as they set up her shrine. They built a small building and one of the women sculpted a statue of my mother's likeness. They burned incense and they blessed the building in her name, begging her to keep her demon protector at bay. They planted her favorite flowers around the hut and the families took it in turns to care for the flowers." Chloe looks up, her face red with shed tears, "That shrine is still there today. I made of my mother a minor deity. I have monitored that shrine and I go there every year. I leave a gift so they know the demon watches still. I think this year I will stay to see what happens when they find my gift."

Scarlett says, "Holy shit. I didn't know it had been like that. I am so sorry. Would you like company this year? What do you leave so they know it was you?"

Chloe laughs, "Chocolate and books. They were my mom's favorite things in the world and what she was never allowed to have when she was with my father. He didn't want his women getting too smart and possibly thinking they were better than him."

"That seems to be a running thing with men, always concerned about whether or not someone else is better than them and how they can drag that person down so they won't be anymore. Admittedly, it is women and all other genders too. I just get more of it from men."

Scarlett nods, "Amen. Now, Chloe, you answer about having company on your trip when you are good and ready. Back to Mikael. You are getting visited by his ghost?"

"Um, I don't think so? Helen seemed to think it was probably he had partnered up with a witch."

"Hmm, well, I think until he provides us with some more concrete evidence, we should go with it is a haunting." Scarlett shrugs, "Maybe Mikael is haunting you because he has thought he owned you for centuries."

I want to argue the point but what if she is right? What if he is just haunting me because he thinks he owns me? "I don't know. It doesn't feel like a haunting, but maybe it is?"

Chloe, her face wiped clean of tears, sniffles a bit and says, "Either way, you should be cautious. We want to keep you around. However, I have a date. Eason wants to take me out to some opera thing. I'll be back tomorrow night after the opera. Tonight he has other surprises for me. Have fun and be safe you two. Bye!"

She hefts her basket and heads for her room. Scarlett hefts her basket and asks me, "Do you have plans tonight?"

"Nah. Tonight was lessons night and I never know what is going to happen so I try not to plan other things. It works better that way. Why? Do you want to do something?"

"Well, I haven't spent much time with you lately. I hoped maybe we could Netflix and chill."

"I like it. Now, my question is, which version of chill do you mean?"

"Both."

"I like it." I giggle and waggle my brows at her, "Let's do it."

She laughs, "Chloe is about to leave so we will have the house to ourselves, let's go down to the living room. The couch is good for cuddles and the tv is the best."

I wait while she drops her basket in her room and grabs a blanket. It's funny, we don't really feel temperature changes for the most part but snuggling up under a blanket is still the most comforting feeling.

The movie we picked isn't great and Scarlett asks, "What else did his mom say? You said the predictions were spooky."

I shift a bit so I can look at her while I speak, "Well, she said that I need to keep my heart open or risk becoming what is after me. Oh, and not to be taken by the demon of the light. Her voice got especially creepy for that. I swear, it sounded like there was more than just her there. Then talking to Hekate later she told me it was love that would keep me trying to do better."

Scarlett shivers, "Fuck. Ok. That is pretty creepy and a lot of pressure for you."

I nod, "Yeah. Then she, came back? Said goodbye to Leonidas and died. I head out for the nurses station to tell them she passed and give him a few minutes alone with her. They tell me she sat up in bed and just stared, turning to look at the door and be disappointed every time someone came in that wasn't me. They were so unsurprised that she passed. And they said crazy shit like that happens there all the time. I don't think I could do that job. Not with the creep factor they are dealing with."

Scarlett shakes her head in agreement, eyes wide, "No fucken way. Nurses deal with way more garbage than they should have to anyway, then throw in a creep factor? Fuck no. I am glad there are people that are strong enough to do it, but I am not one of them."

A slow grin spreading across my face I say, "You know, this movie is kind of lame and I don't want to talk about creepy predictions or overworked nurses any more. How do you feel about going upstairs, getting naked, and maybe railing each other for a while?"

She grins back, "I think that sounds like an excellent idea."

Six

Jasmine

I am nearly finished with the book I have been reading all day when I hear the noise. Scarlett just went out a few hours ago and Chloe isn't due back till later. But it's the last damn chapter! Maybe if I ignore it they will go away? I get through a couple more sentences and I can't do it. I grab a receipt and slip it between the pages before I set the book down on the table and leave the room to find what idiot is disturbing my book time.

Whoever they are, they will pay.

I hear this little mouse tiptoeing about toward the back of the down stairs. I know that it won't be anyone I know. In case it is someone that is a vampire or other creature that could be more difficult for me I throw a shield up over myself. That at least, I have down even if the constant whole house protection still defeats me. As I pad down the hall I see a human walking softly as he leaves Chloe's office. He is heading for the next door so I lean against the door jamb and wait for him. He never sees me until he opens the door and I whisper, "Boo." He jumps as he sees me and makes his second bad choice. His eyes travel down my body and back up before he says, "I sure am sorry I'm going to have to kill you. Maybe we can have some fun before I send you to meet your maker."

I smile at him, "Tell me, did you case this house before you broke in?Learn anything about the inhabitants?"

He laughs as he tries to put his hands on me. His laughter trickles away as he realizes I am not there and he never saw me move. I reach out and tap his shoulder, "So you have no idea what you have walked into here?"

He pulls a knife out of his belt, "Bitch, I got a job to do." He stabs forward with the knife, putting his whole body into it. I step to the side, snatching the knife with one hand while the other shoves him into a wall. He leaves a few dents on the wall, I'll have to get Leonidas to come fix them.

Tossing the knife away I grab him by the throat and let my fangs descend as I bring his face near to mine and I whisper to him, "Let's go have some fun sugar." His screams are frankly disappointing. I take him back to the living area I had been sitting in and ask, "What job are you here to do?"

He never pauses in his screaming and sniveling. I can't even tell what he is trying to say. I give him a shake but he just screams louder. I bite him and drink until he shuts up because I just can't stand all the noise and snot. Ugh. He stills and silence falls over the house again. I release the artery I have been drinking from and give the wounds a lick to heal them. He isn't the best tasting I have ever had but not the worst either. Letting him drop to the floor I enjoy the sound of silence for a moment. I do feel really sated and that is nice. I forget that the stored blood isn't as potent as the fresh from the source version.

With a sigh I lean down and start rifling through his pockets. He doesn't have much on him. Some drives he stole from Chloe's office and his wallet. I snort, novice. What kind of moron takes his whole wallet to a job where he was sent to kill someone? I open his wallet and I freeze as the scent of Mikael hits me. Dropping the wallet on the dead man I suddenly wish I hadn't been so hasty. I set the drives on the table as I take my seat again and drink deeply from my wine glass, watching the body that has left only more questions.

Seven

Mikael

Vigo enters my office his head down and his movements jerky. Hake raises a brow and I shrug as I wait for Vigo to approach and get whatever it is out. He stops a few feet away, "Sir, I— we have a problem."

"I can see that Vigo. What is the problem?"

"The, the human. He insisted on being paid before he left. I paid him because I knew this was important but now he hasn't checked in and he seems to be… to be missing." I am up from my seat and grabbing Vigo by the hair, yanking his head back so I can see his face.

Look into his wide eyes as I say, "What do you mean he seems to be missing?"

"Please, please sir, he hasn't left the house. She was home and I was waiting for him to leave after he finished. He hasn't left the house. I—I fear that he is dead."

Rage paints my vision red and I fling Vigo across the room. He lands and I am there, yanking him up by the shirt and shaking him, "How could you pay him before he left? Now she knows!" I slap him once and then again. "You gave him money from my house! Sending the human was meant to confuse her further!"

Remembering that Hake is across the room watching and listening I drop Vigo to the ground where he lands in a heap. "Get your ass out there and watch for the body to leave the house. Follow the body and check the wallet, if it is still with the body. See if the money is there and if the wallet smells like anything other than him and money that came from me. Do you think you can handle that Vigo?"

"Yes sir, thank you sir. I will do as you command. Thank you. Can I get you anything before I leave?"

"No Vigo. Just go."

I return to my seat and pick up my drink. Hake murmurs, "Difficult to find good help for special tasks these days."

I nod with a grimace, "It is. He excels as an assistant in so many ways but things like this, I am afraid he simply does not have the aptitude for it. This is a short term issue though and now that you and I are coming to an agreement, I feel certain that my life will go back to being quiet, as it was before she came into my life. Now, you are up to date on what I have been working on, tell me what you have planned next for her? Since the appearance of myself is only working slowly."

"I am going to arrange to meet her. Read her. I will know more after that. We should continue with the shades of you. That does seem to be making her unsure of herself. The more off balance she is the easier it will be to screw with her in other ways, making her vulnerable to attacks that will rid you of her presence in a more permanent manner. Or, make her your pet. Either way."

I lift my glass to take a deep draw of the liquor within. I don't fancy the idea of Hake meeting her but, he is likely correct. If he reads her magically he will likely be able to get much deeper than I was able to get to know her in the short time I had her in my home. "I think that will be a good assignment for you. Find out more about her by scanning her magically. I am sure you will find much she kept hidden from me."

Hake raises a brow and stands, "Very well. I will go and work at seeing where will be the best place to find her and read her. Don't worry about escorting me out, I know the way now."

"Very well. I look forward to hearing good news of your success."

Eight

Jasmine

I am still staring at this stupid corpse when Chloe and Scarlett arrive and when they walk in the room.

Chloe is the first one to recover, "Jasmine! We don't bring kills home ever! What were you thinking?"

My brows drop into a scowl at her words, "I didn't bring him here. He broke in to kill me for someone else."

Scarlett's head whips around to look at me, "What did you say? Isn't that a human?"

"It is. He said he was here to kill me and that it was a job. He was hired to kill me."

Chloe says, "Shit, I'm sorry Jas. I wasn't thinking. Of course you wouldn't bring one home. What idiot would send a human to kill you?"

"His wallet is just there," I point in the general area to the left of the body where it landed when I threw it, "smell the money in it."

Scarlett snatches up the wallet and Chloe is next to her when she opens it. Both of them exclaim, "Mikael!"

Scarlett meets my eyes, "I'm sorry we didn't take it more seriously when you told us he was back and fucking with you. We just thought he was dead. Like, no coming back-from-it dead and maybe you were missing the idea of him."

Chloe nods in agreement, "We have both had our fair share of trouble with our own exes and makers, yours is all rolled up into one giant pain in the ass package. I am so sorry we didn't take you more seriously. I promise it won't happen again."

I wipe something from my eye, "It's ok. Now stop before you make me cry."

Scarlett drops the wallet, "We need to figure out how to make Mikael forever dead. This motherfucker doesn't know when to quit."

"No! I don't want to kill him!"

Scarlett scowls at me, "Why the fuck not? He keeps trying to kill you, control you, and hurt your friends when you don't comply! Killing him is just the most logical fucking option!"

Chloe chimes in with, "Fucking hell! Even if you aren't that mad at him, I still haven't forgiven him for putting us in a cage. A fucking cage Jas! I cannot begin to describe the shit that brought up for me. We cannot let him continue on with his bullshit."

I look away, "I'm sorry. I'm so sorry. I—if there is any other way to stop him I don't want to kill him. Can you please just promise me we will at least look at other options before we go with killing him?"

I watch as they share a look. Chloe says, "We will look at them. But they have to be permanent. None of us should have to live in fear of his stupid ass. Not me, not Scarlett, not you or anyone else."

"I agree. Thank you. For trying for me. Now, what do we do with this body? I've never had one in my house before. Disposal methods are usually closer at hand."

"We call a service. Most of the time when this happens, it was some moron breaking in to rob a place. It has happened often enough that we, vampires as a whole, contracted out for it. It isn't cheap but we don't generally mind. Being so long lived, money isn't usually a problem after the first few decades."

"Who? How? What?"

Chloe laughs, "Scarlett, why don't you go call them and I'll explain our mob ties to her?"

Scarlett laughs as she pulls out her phone, she walks over and pats my arm, "Don't worry, it will be all right." Then she leaves the room while tapping at her phone before putting it to her ear.

Chloe sits next to me, "So what do you know about the mob?"

"Um, not a lot. I mean, did they like, give vampires a hotline or something? Because that would be a little hilarious."

"Well, no. What they did do is make a world-wide agreement to provide the services. Now, the cost varies from place to place. We have one contact per area. Basically, when we arrive we have to find a gang member, usually is not difficult once you know what to look for, and then we ask for the special services liaison. Or the closest approximation in the local language. They meet with you and the person affirms that you are eligible for the services and they give you the number for that area. The only requirement to be eligible is being a vampire. It is always better to meet them in person at least once before calling. You get better rates that way."

"Shit. I guess so. Um, will one or both of you introduce me?"

"Of course! We forget that you are still new…" Chloe stares off into the distance, "Son of a bitch! That's how he is doing it! That's why you knew he wasn't dead! Why you are so loathe to kill him! He is your maker!"

"Um, what?"

Scarlett walks in and Chloe says, "The makers bond!"

Scarlett smacks her forehead, "How could we forget about that? Why didn't he use that to find the house though?"

"That fucker probably felt it was beneath him." Chloe snarls, "Which is why he hired people."

I hear Hekate's voice, "I was blocking him then. I couldn't do it forever, but I was allowed to do it for a time while you needed the protection from him finding you."

"Oh. Okay." Chloe and Scarlett look at me like I have grown another head, "Sorry. Hekate just spoke to me and she said that he couldn't use the bond to find me because she was blocking him from doing so. She couldn't make it permanent, but she did it for as long as she could. So, am I understanding correctly? This is why he can find me when he wants to throw his shade out at me to harass me?"

Scarlett shrugs, "Probably? It is definitely why you knew he isn't dead."

Chloe wraps her arms around me and hugs me tight, "I am so sorry. If we don't find a way to keep him under wraps killing him is going to hurt you." She releases me but grabs my shoulders and looks me in the eye, "I know it will suck but we will be here for you. Also," she glances at Scarlett who turns away looking really uncomfortable, "Scarlett doesn't like me telling you this because it almost forces things for you but, the more attached to other people you are the easier it is to survive a maker dying before the link has faded. Now, the good thing is, that the attachments don't have to be romantic."

"Tell her the rest Chlo."

"It works so much better if the attachments are romantic. Friendships work, but they take more time to build to that level. Having at least one love interest ups your chances of survival by a ridiculous amount."

"What do you mean survival? Is it possible I could die if we kill him now?"

Chloe nods and drops her hands into her lap, "It is. New vampires will most often die if their maker does early on. The rate of survival..."

Scarlett turns to face us, "It isn't good Jasmine. Mostly they die. We don't talk about it much and mostly makers will lie rather than tell their fledgling and, well, in general we just try to keep it quiet. Most vampires don't get themselves killed while they have a new vampire under their care. And even less will attempt to kill a new vampire in their care."

"Well, how many of them have had three um, interests?"

Scarlett laughs, "Not very many, not very many at all."

"I mean, if it keeps me alive, I think I could maybe take the possibility of future heartbreak over now death. Probably?" I flop back on the couch to stare up at the ceiling, "This is so much. Why can't anything just be easy? I mean, I can't even kill a dude breaking into our home without it being a whole damn situation. And now I can either take my chances or try to push my relationships into places I'm not ready for. Fuck me."

Nine

Jasmine

I put the finishing touches on my makeup and exit the bathroom. Picking up my phone I see that Leonidas should be here any time now. I shove my phone into a small bag I picked up to go with the dress for his mother's funeral. One last check in the mirror and I head downstairs. I haven't been a vampire all that long but it still feels odd to be going out in public during the day. I have avoided it all this time with few exceptions and now we are intentionally going out.

His mother's funeral is worth it though. She seemed like a really nice woman that had an exceptionally difficult life. I make it to the bottom of the stairs and I still have a few minutes that I spend pacing the entry. I like the sound my heels make and I haven't been vampire long enough to not feel some anxiety about this. I know his step-grandfather was a disgusting trash fire of a person, I have to wonder if perhaps some of the other family members are as well.

I hear his truck pull up outside and I go to meet him. I would just as soon get this over with. He is just stepping out of his truck when I open the door. He walks around and opens his passenger door for me, holding it as I get in. He leans in and touches his forehead to mine briefly before stepping back and closing the door. I watch as he gets in and starts the truck. Backing out of the drive he tells me, "We are going to my house for now, the limo will meet us there. We have our own. My mother set all this up so long ago, but apparently she knew you would be there and that I would need space from the rest of the family."

"Your mother is an amazing person and I am glad I had the opportunity to meet her. How are you holding up?"

"Better now. A lot of the family is mad about everything. They are mad that they haven't been allowed to go paw through her things. Mad that her will won't be read until tomorrow. Really mad that I posted some of my employees at the house she used to live in so that they couldn't just break in. They are all just hungry for her money."

"Her money? What?"

"Mom was pretty well off. I paid for her stay in the nursing home because I wanted to, not because it would have hurt her finances. She was always pretty frugal in her spending but she made a lot of money with her gifts once she was away from her step-father."

"That is awesome. So she never had to worry about being trapped financially again. I love that."

Leonidas chuckles, "She did say something like that a lot. She would be fresh from a reading where she had been telling another young woman how to get herself out of a situation and she would wish that there was a way for her to get that message out to all women. She said women should never depend on a man or anyone else for their basic needs of food and shelter. As she got older and the world changed she amended it to people, but when she first started saying it she didn't know there was more than just the two sexes."

"I wish I could have known her back then. She probably would have had some sound advice for me."

He nods as we pull into his driveway. The limo is already there and waiting so we move from one vehicle to the next and our journey continues. In the limo he is pensive and seems quiet so I let him be. He reaches over and takes my hand, holding it the rest of the trip. The driver pulls up in front of a grand old church, waiting to get to the drop off area and I look at Leonidas, my eyes wide, "Can we go in there?"

He barks a laugh and clears his throat, "Yes, we'll be fine in there. No worries. Churches were never an issue and neither were crosses. He didn't teach you much of anything did he?"

"Not a lot, no. And some of what he did teach I forgot in light of things like him trying to kill me."

"I can see how that would blur things a bit."

"Plus he was really focused on making sure I kept other things secret."

The limo driver pulls under the covered area and steps out to open the door for us. As I exit he hands Leonidas a card with a phone number on it and tells him to call if he would like to leave for the graveside earlier and that he is at his disposal for the night.

Leonidas asks, "What do you mean for the night?"

The driver looks around and smiles revealing fangs, "Your mother hired me specifically for you because I am one of you with a really great sunblock recipe. I'll see you when you are finished in there. I'll be first in line after the hearse if you wait for the procession."

Leonidas nods, "Thank you. We will likely wait for the procession."

I am just amazed as we go inside. Amazed by his mother thinking so much through and finding us a vamp limo driver. Plus, this gives me a way to go out in the day time! It gives us all a way. I have to talk to this driver after we get out of here. I wonder if I can trade him for his recipe? We enter the main cathedral and I am stunned. I have never been in a church so opulent. I mean, wow. There is stained glass everywhere, the pews look traditional but with really plush padding. The raised dias where her coffin lies is huge and covered in a deep burgundy carpet. I am in awe as we walk up to view his mother.

She looks so peaceful. I hope wherever she is now, she is at peace. We don't stay at her side for long. For one, there is a line behind us. For two, vampires can't cry in mixed company. People see blood tears leaking down your face and they tend to get rather hysterical. The usher shows us directly to the first pew and insists that it is reserved for Leonidas and one. The rest of the family is shown to a first pew on the other side, and the second pews on both sides. After that it appears that the other mourners are her friends and clients. Most of them stop by where Leonidas and I are seated to express their condolences. They are all really nice. I smell more than one vampire and multiple witches. Even a few wolves. There are some humans in the mix as well, which is more along the lines of what I expected. I never would have thought I would get an introduction to a large part of the magical community at his mother's funeral. This is wild.

The viewing ends as everyone is seated and the priest enters. He does his ceremony and says a lot of the usual trite things, then at the very end he gets choked up and says, "She will be dearly missed by all who truly knew her."

I hear someone behind me say in a loud whisper, "Oh get on with it old man! She wasn't that special!"

I turn to glare at that person and find that every other person not family has done the same. They realize that about the same time I do and glare around the room defiantly. I see more than a few nods that would have terrified me as a human and I smile as I turn away. I think this problem will be sorted without me.

An usher appears to escort Leonidas and I to the side door and our waiting limo. His mother's casket is being wheeled out ahead of us. I hear grumbles from the family pews about why we are going first but I ignore them since I figure Leonidas probably doesn't want that scene to happen right here behind his mother's coffin.

The usher opens the limo door and holds it while we get in. Leonidas remains silent as we watch his mother's coffin being loaded into the hearse. They are so gentle and maybe the rest of the family doesn't appreciate it but I think Leonidas does. I see tears tracking down his face and I pull out some tissues. I am thankful he is wearing all black and I hold onto the tissues until we enter the graveyard. Leonidas tells me that the building next to it is the old church, that they bought a new building as the congregation grew but they have kept the building for administration persons and such since the graveyard isn't something they want to move. I hand him the tissues and he looks at them like he doesn't understand what they are for until I tell him, "Your face was leaking a little sweetie. We can't let your family see the blood tears."

Realization spreads across his face and he wipes at it with large, ineffective strokes. I cover his hand with mine and gently take the tissues from him. I wipe his face, and into his collar a bit. Once he is good I touch my forehead to his briefly, and he lets out a shuddering exhale. "Just a little longer and then we can leave here with our driver. I know it's hard, but you have to be strong a lit— wait. I can glamour you! Helen taught me that! Hold on. Go ahead and let the tears flow, I need to see them."

He does, they run as soon as he lets his guard down a little. I work the spell the way that Helen taught me, seeing it the way I want everyone else to see it as I set my magic in place. As I finish up I tap on the partition between us and the driver. He lowers it and I ask him, "What color are his tears?"

His brows drop as I ask and then they raise near to his hairline before he says, "They look like regular tears! How did you do that? I know people that would pay for that. So many vamps that can't go to a loved one's funeral because of the tears."

"We can talk about that later. I want to talk to you anyway about the sunscreen. I have questions."

"I thought you already had it. Will you two be all right out there?"

"We'll be fine. And we will talk after, for now we need to finish this."

The graveside service is long and boring. I hear grumbles from the rest of the family but they are keeping them quiet so I am ignoring them. I know I am not the only one hearing them but I think this family doesn't realize the kind of danger they are putting themselves in. There are entirely too many people here that cannot cry for one reason or another and will happily channel their feelings into rage to help themselves maintain. That rage may not dissipate just because the funeral ends and they can go somewhere private to mourn her.

The priest ends his speech and she is lowered into the ground. Leonidas pulls a single rose out of his jacket and tosses it in with her. We step a little away from the graveside and he speaks with the priest, placing a large donation check into his hands and telling him how grateful he is that he was willing to provide the service for his mother.

The priest nods and his eyes flash so quickly that I think I imagined it until he says, "Every one of us is beloved by our deities, even those with differences. Your mother was beloved by the community and one of the best women I know. If you should need anything Leonidas, please do not hesitate to call on me."

I scent the air and realize that the priest here is a shifter of some sort. I guess he can sense or see the questions in my mind because he smiles at me and says with a wink, "I have a love of bears, even got a tattoo of one when I was a young man. And what is your name?"

Leonidas says, "I'm sorry, I should have introduced her, this is Jasmine."

His eyes widen and he says, "The Jasmine?"

I look at Leonidas and he shrugs before saying, "Not sure what you mean father?"

The priest looks around and whispers, "The one your mother saw in her visions."

I nod, "Yes. That would be me. Nice to meet you Father Neally."

The priest says, "Wonderful! You must come see me soon. I have things for you. Information as well. I can't say more here," he reaches into his robes and pulls out a card he promptly presses into my hand, "call me. It is very important that we speak soon."

I take the card and slip it into my bag. "I'll call you soon for an appointment."

Leonidas is as curious as I am at this point but his family is now behind us waiting to speak with the priest so we take our leave and go to speak with the group of people that have been patiently standing off to the side who wave and whisper from a good bit away that they would like to speak with us. I know his family didn't hear them but we walk over and I can feel their eyes on us even as I hear Father Neally leading them further away from us.

The group consists of multiple magical species. A vampire, wolf shifter, witch, and something else are standing at the front of the group looking like spokespeople. The vampire takes the lead as we stop in front of them, "We couldn't help but overhear your conversation with Father Neally. Alena was our friend. Leonidas, we are deeply sorry for your loss. She was an amazing person and a gifted seer. Which is how we know about you, Jasmine." He says as everyone focuses on me. "She told us a great many things before she left this place. We would like to meet with you soon to talk about them. We realize that now is not—" He stops speaking as the sound of some one stomping draws closer and a hand lands on Leonidas shoulder. The fingers turn white as the person tries to spin him around.

Leonidas turns to look at the person with an eyebrow raised, "Can I help you Tony?"

Tony removes his hand and puts his finger in Leonidas's face, "How dare you bring one of your street women here! To your mother's funeral! My sister deserved better than that!"

"So we are uncle and nephew today? Not half brothers? Fine. *Uncle*. You do not get to question anything about who I bring to my mother's funeral and you can shove your assumptions directly up your ass. If you need," he rolls his shoulders and smiles, "help getting it there, I would be happy to offer my assistance."

"How dare you! Threatening violence at my sister's funeral! I ought to have you arrested like the criminal you are. But," he smoothes back his hair, "I don't want to further besmirch your mother's memory. Now, who are the dirty drifters you have installed at your mother's home? You can't keep us out of there forever, we are entitled to mementos of her, she was dear to us as well. And the reading of her will is tomorrow." He looks smug as he says the last.

Leonidas barks a laugh, "As if you cared. I know you haven't been to see her in years Tony. It is well documented. Also, she said you would try this and to tell you it won't work. But you go for it. The people are none of your business."

"I have reason to believe that she left me that house in her will, did you know she contracted another lawyer?"

From the back of the crowd behind us a voice says, "No she didn't."

Tony's fists go to his hips, "How the fuck would you know weirdo? She was my sister, not yours."

A slim and slight man with an aura of power surrounding him walks up to stand in front of the four we were speaking to and says, "I am her attorney. I have held her accounts for many years and I personally go over her accountants' work every month. I can assure you, no money went to another lawyer. And her only will is the one that I filed. If you seek to take this to court I will sue you for fraud and seek charges against you and anyone that aids you in this farce."

I put a hand over my mouth to cover my smile but Tony sees it any way and swings at me. Leonidas catches his arm in a crushing grip as he says, "Apologize to the lady. Now."

Tony starts yowling about his arm and Leonidas calmly starts turning it. Tony quickly realizes that Leonidas is going to break it and shouts, "I'm sorry! I'm sorry! I didn't mean anything by it! Let goooooo! I did what you asked!"

Leonidas releases his arm and he cradles it to his body, "You'll pay for that! That was assault! I have witnesses! I'll take everything from you!"

Leonidas laughs and gestures at the people standing with us, watching silently as all this goes on, "What do you think these fine people are but witnesses to the fact that I acted in defense of another?"

Tony stomps off cradling his arm and yelling, "You will pay for this Leonidas! I'll take everything from you! Just you wait!"

The man that proclaimed himself Alena's attorney puts his hand out to Leonidas saying, "Hello. I meant to introduce myself after everyone else had spoken to you but it seemed prudent that I step forward then. My name is Rinfell. Steven Rinfell. Here is my card," he pulls one out of his pocket and passes it to Leonidas, "I am the attorney that will be reading your mother's will. Please do continue to ensure that no one from your family enters the house. It would be... messy if they did."

I can't help myself and I blurt, "Messy?"

He smiles a particularly evil smile, "Yes. Very messy. She had it arranged that way and as you can see," he gestures behind him, "she knew some very interesting people with talents outside the usual. She also knew how awful her family would be and took precautions."

I can't help but giggle, "Maybe you should have the boys leave the house and let them break in." Leonidas smiles a real smile for the first time since his mother passed and it melts my heart so I continue on, "We could warn them about Alena's curse and then when they see it in action they will be terrified for the rest of their extra short lives."

Leonidas chuckles, "Why would they be extra short?"

I quit smiling as I say, "Because then I will hunt them all down and make sure their lives are cut short."

Leonidas laughs out loud and Rinfell laughs too before saying, "Leonidas, do make sure you bring her to the reading. She is entertaining and I think I could really get along with a woman so vicious as her, reminds me of one of my own daughters. And, the reading involves her as well."

"What?" I say, my confusion apparent on my face, "What do you mean it involves me? I only met her a couple of times. She is a wonderful lady but she shouldn't be including me in her will."

Rinfell says, "Yes, she said you would feel that way and that you were to put those feelings aside as there are many things you don't know. I expect to see you there, Ms. Felton. Don't make me come find you."

I can feel the power rolling off him and I tell him I'll be there. He says his goodbyes and takes his leave, having done what he came to do. The vampire that had been speaking before being interrupted by Tony says, "I am so sorry that this is all such a mess. My name is Caden by the way. We," he gestures at the people still there with him, "still very much need to speak with you Jasmine. I am aware of where to find you, if you would like us to meet you at your home. If you would prefer elsewhere you may call me," he holds up his phone, "I can share my contact information with your phone if you would pull it out to accept it?"

I nod and take my phone out of my purse, the screen is lit up with a request to accept Caden's contact information. I touch the screen to accept it and he smiles. "Thank you Jasmine. My colleagues," he gestures at the three standing next to him, "Frank, Lacey, and Nia; we all look forward to seeing you very soon. The rest do too, but we are elected as spokespersons currently."

"Um, this is a little much. Give me a few days, my schedule is filling up in ways I didn't expect so I will need to make room. I have lessons that I refuse to miss and other lessons that will find me wherever I may be, she would not be happy if I didn't show. We want her happy. So, I promise I will call and get together with you as soon as is possible, don't hunt me down."

Caden chuckles, "Understood. May we ask who your mentors are? Out of curiosity only."

"Well, one is Helen Bastille. Love her, she is so patient with me. The other, well, she hasn't said not to tell anyone and she did appear before the entire vampire council so I guess it is ok to tell you, my other mentor is Hekate."

Faces that were pale to begin with grow even more pale. Caden clears his throat and cleans an ear with his finger, "I'm sorry, I thought you said Hekate, I must have heard incorrectly."

From behind me her voice says, "You heard correctly Caden. I am teaching her some of my more..." she looks up as is searching for the right phrasing, "fun tricks."

Her smile is wide and mildly frightening. Caden swallows, "I see. Well, you certainly would not want to miss a lesson with her as I am sure they are enlightening."

Hekate touches Leonidas's arm and tell him, "I am sorry for your loss. Your mother was an amazing human and the world is a little darker for the loss of her light."

Caden looks shocked that Hekate cares about Alena's death. She looks him in the eye and says, "Did you think she wouldn't be on my radar? I think you might be surprised at just who I do monitor." Caden's eyes get round and he is so pale I am almost concerned for him.

I hear Hekate start laughing and I see her fade away from the corner of my eye. I look back to Caden, "So yeah. She knows where I am. And I guess she approves of you so I will definitely see you all soon."

After Hekate left the conversation moved to Alena and her life. Everyone had warm memories of her to share. It left me wishing I had known her better and feeling like she will have more of a hand in my life to come.

We make our way to the limo where our driver waits. He opens the door for us and once we are in he closes it and gets in front. The middle partition lowers as he starts the car and asks us if we have a place we would like to go. Leonidas has his head leaned back and his eyes closed but he shakes his head no when I look toward him so I ask, "Do you mind driving us around while you and I talk about sunscreen and things?"

He smiles, "I love that idea. Makes us much more difficult to listen to and lets me drive which I enjoy. I'll take us down I-40 a ways, some nice scenery that way."

I sit back and take Leonidas's hand, he squeezes mine gently and lays his head on my shoulder. We get on the interstate and the driver says, "My name is Nathan. What's yours?"

"Jasmine. Would you tell me about this sunscreen? Is it a widely known trick?"

He grins, "No, it isn't. I only know of about three dozen or so vampires that know the recipe. A number of them were here today. The thing is, even the humans that volunteer as feeders for vampires, they won't recognize a vampire unless they are wanted by the council and flyers are out. But I mean, changing the way you look is easy. So going out during the day is pretty safe and if you get caught by someone that could cause problems you either kill them or let them in on the sunblock. There is a thing with the sunblock. A curse of sorts. See, the recipe was invented a long time ago by a witch that had taken a vampire lover. She didn't mind becoming a vampire to be with her lover forever but she loved watching the day begin. So she created the sunblock recipe. But, she was concerned that certain vampires would misuse it. She set the recipe with magic and made it so that if the person using it was doing things that would expose the community or doing great harm without cause, it would poison them. I don't know the mechanics of what she did, but I have seen it work. Some vampires I won't name gave it to certain other vamps they suspected were committing certain atrocities. The vamps they gave it to died miserable deaths. I didn't even know we could be poisoned but I guess with magic..." He shrugs.

"I love that. What an ingenious idea! I can't imagine how she managed to put her requirements on the recipe but now I want to reverse engineer it in case I ever have something so cool to use it on."

"Yes. Now, what you did today with the, what did you call it? Glamour?"

"Oh, yeah. It is just a little illusion meant to disguise a thing. Most witches use it for beauty or disguise but, making the tears of a vampire clear so he can feel his emotions at his mother's funeral, I felt like that was a need. I could probably put the spell on some water that could be put in an atomizer and sprayed at the person. I think most witches could do that. It isn't a difficult spell or even a really powerful one."

"Ah, but they may not be able to figure it out without a boost or they may not have the time to figure it out. Seeing what has already been created can provide a way to see what was done and create similar without much effort."

"Indeed. Well, I can certainly make one or three up for you if you would like. I would really like to have the recipe for the sunblock. That would make my life a lot easier."

His eyes get sly in the mirror, "Because it would make it easier to get away with what you are already doing?"

"Well, yes. I have carte blanche for it but I worry for my friends who don't necessarily have a goddess to go to bat at the council for them. Basically if anyone reports me to the council they aren't getting far, but my friends don't have that protection."

Nathan nods, "I see. And I see why a goddess is backing you. You don't have to worry about the council at all anymore, do you?"

I shake my head no, "They have a file on me that says to let me be ever since Hekate showed up at my hearing."

Nathan laughs, "I bet some of them shit themselves over that. She is fucking fierce. I will pass the recipe on to you. You all can carry it around with you and pretend to be wearing it. But, would you mind sharing your secret with me?"

Leonidas opens his eyes and lifts his head to look at me. Nathan sees this and my apprehension, "If you don't wish to tell me, I will understand. I would also add that I can keep a secret if that helps any."

I look at Leonidas and he shrugs, "I do know he can keep secrets. I've known him for a very long time and I had no idea until today that he had dealings with my mother."

Nathan chuckles, "She was a magnificent woman and she is missed. She was also much more crafty than most people would guess. Which can be a bit of a shock if you were her son and not necessarily aware of how much interaction she had with the magical community at large."

Leonidas looks out the window, "I did not realize there were so many or that she had been watching for Jasmine for so very long. That part was more shocking than so many of the magical community loving her."

Nathan nods as he pulls off on an exit to turn us around, "She was happy you would go on as a vampire. Did she tell you that?"

Leonidas' lips lift in a sad half smile, "She hinted at it. I think she didn't want to tell me out right back then because I was also running a small gang that was less than interested in legalities or niceties of any kind really. Probably didn't want to seem like she was endorsing that."

Nathan chuckles, "No, she wouldn't want that. She had very definite ideas about right and wrong. She knew what happened to her step-father though and she wasn't the least bit sorry or mad about it though she spent a long time thinking she should be."

Leonidas watches Nathan in the rearview, "I didn't realize she knew that."

I look between the both of them, "Knew what?"

Nathan raises his browns and Leonidas nods so he says, "Knew that Leonidas rid the world of a disgusting piece of filth that continually hurt his mother and was Leonidas' birth father. The entire community silently cheered you for that."

"You all knew?"

"We did, and she made each of us promise not to be the one to kill him. She said the one that would do it would do it at the right time. Now, we are nearly back to town. Would you all like to drive around more, go to a place? Tonight is your night."

Leonidas looks to me, "Would you like to go to the observatory?"

I smile wide, "You know I would."

"Take us to the observatory please, Nathan."

⁓

Jasmine

The funeral was only yesterday but it seems like weeks have passed. Nathan was fun to talk with and he helped me cheer Leonidas a bit before we went to my house and Nathan gave me his card so I could contact him once I had the glamour sorted.

Tonight is lessons with Helen so I am going to ask her to help me with it. I think she will support the idea. My phone starts ringing as I drive and I hit the button on my steering wheel to answer it. "Hello."

"Hi, Jasmine, it's Sebastian."

"Hey Sebastian! How are you? Seems like I never see you now that we have our place back. You guys could come by you know?"

"Heh, that's actually what I called about. I'd like to see you again, take you out on a date if you would be interested in that?

"Oh. I—I would be. But I need to lay out some facts and ground rules for you. I know we had sex before and you and Leonidas had a little rivalry going on for a hot minute. I need you to know before I go any further that I am seeing Leonidas and Scarlett. They are both aware that I am seeing them and I fully intend to keep seeing both of them even if you and I keep seeing each other. All of those relationships are inclusive of sex, though we aren't all having sex together at this point in time. Are you good with all that? There can't be a rivalry, I have too much going on right now."

"I hadn't really considered that. I understand where you are coming from and I still want to be more of a part of your life. And I would still like to take you out on a date soon. I can't promise it will work out, I have never been a part of something quite like this. I want to try though. I haven't been able to get you out of my mind Jasmine."

"I am one of a kind," I laugh, "but, are you sure? I know this is asking a lot. I would like to see where it would go with you but I need them too."

"I am sure that I want to at least try and that I won't lie to you about my feelings at any point. If I get uncomfortable for some reason, you will know about it before it gets out of hand."

"That's all I can ask for. Yes, I would very much like to go out with you. When would you like to do this?"

"Could I see you tonight?"

"Yes, Leonidas has work tonight and Scarlett is off with Chloe playing their favorite game, mind if I text you when I get done with my lessons so we can meet up?"

"I would very much like that. See you then."

"See you then."

I hit the button to end the call as I pull into the parking lot. This is so wild. I never could have imagined a situation like this in my old life. Parking the car I hop out and wander thru the book store. I've been in here countless times and the scents still delight me. Slipping into the back hall I meet Helen at the door to the training room, "Oh good! You're here!"

"Am I late?"

"No, I am eager to get started. I plan to work on the house shielding with you. I thought about what you said, that your room mates wouldn't appreciate not being able to move freely in or out. I have figured out the fix. You need to key the spell to allow certain people to move in and out as they please, and if they decide to bring others in they only need to be touching the person or persons. Does that sound like something that would work for you all? It would be the same for you."

"I think it would work. It sounds better than anything I came up with. But, I also have a question."

Helen smiles so big I think her face might split, "A question? All this time you have just absorbed what I taught you and not many if any questions. Tell me, what is it you want to do? I know you must be looking to do something!" She claps her hands together in front of her and leans forward in her chair as she waits for my answer.

I wish I had something more complex to ask her about now. I feel like I am going to let her down with this, but it will ensure the safety of my friends. "Well, Leonidas' mother died recently and yesterday we attended her funeral. It was a great strain on Leonidas, trying not to let his emotions show so I put a glamour on him." I go on to explain the rest of the story about Nathan and the sunblock and needing it for my friends who have this ability because of me but lack the protection of a goddess. Helen listens so intently and with a scrutiny that is almost uncomfortable.

When I finish she has a tear in her eye and says, "This is what Hekate was talking about. You are going above and beyond for your friends; old, new, and possible. You are a good soul Jasmine. We can do exactly what you told him, and that is most definitely a worthy use for a glamour. All of us magical species, we are somewhat insular. We don't necessarily notice the pain of the other species, because mostly we don't spend a lot of time outside our own kind. Seems we need to do better. If you don't mind, I would like to pass the spell for this around to other witches, there is no reason why we shouldn't have that on offer for vampires simply trying to mourn their loved ones."

"I think that would be a great way to further close the gap between witches and vampires. Let's get to it."

Two hours later we have two spells worked out. The spell to shield my house is ready and is something I can do with relative ease. The glamour spell took more finesse but we got it working. Once we were pretty sure we had it I made myself cry, which wasn't hard to do. I pictured my friends locked up in that cage Mikael had put them in and they flowed. Helen waited long enough for the tears to get half down my face and gave me a spritz. Her happy dance told me all I needed to know. After that I washed it off and she spritzed the other side before I started crying, so we could be sure it would work.

It worked like a charm.

After that we said our goodnights and I headed for my car, eager to text Sebastian. Just as I get in my phone rings and I see it is Leonidas, "Hello! How are you doing? Work going good tonight?"

"Better hearing your voice. Work is going well, we are on target. Tomorrow is the will reading. Are you ready for it?"

"Uh, no. But I guess I will be?"

He chuckles and the sound rolls over me, making me feel warm and happy. "How about I pick you up for it, say about two? The meeting is at three but it is across town from where you live."

"I would love that. The ride over will give me the chance to spend some time with you." I hear Banner in the background calling him to look at something and he doesn't sound happy so I am not surprised when Leonidas says he has to go. "I will see you tomorrow. Hope it's nothing serious."

"Me too. I'm looking forward to seeing you too. Bye." His voice got darker and warmer as he said the last and sent shivers right through me as he ended the call. I go ahead and message Sebastian that I should be home in twenty minutes or so. He immediately texts me back saying he will be there waiting.

Ten

Jasmine

When I get to the house Sebastian is there waiting as promised. I get out of my car and he steps out of the shadows of our porch and asks, "How do you feel about moonlit walks in gardens?"

I look up at the full moon out tonight and I can't remember ever going on a moonlit walk anywhere that I wasn't on guard and concerned for my own welfare. The freedom being a vampire has given me isn't something I think I could ever give up. I look back to Sebastian and find he is standing in front of me, just far enough away that he isn't crowding me or invading my space. Smiling I say, "I think that would be really nice."

"What were you thinking about when you looked up at the moon just now?"

"I was thinking about the freedom of a vampire."

He cocks his head to one side, "Not sure I understand."

"It doesn't matter anyway. Are we going now or?"

He extends his arm, bent at the elbow, "Yes, now. M'lady?"

I take his arm with a grin and he escorts me to his car where he opens the door and holds it while I get in, closing it gently before walking round and getting himself into the driver's seat.

We are cruising through town when I ask him, "How did you get the garden to be open at night?"

He looks away briefly and says, "I donate pretty heavily to the place and I have a seat on the board. Plus, I offered to pay the wages of everyone that worked for the night. Only double. And I made sure it was voluntary."

"Wow. That is fantastic. I am sure they appreciate that."

He turns into a parking lot, "I hope it shows my appreciation enough."

We get out and walk through a lovely building filled with local artwork and he points out certain pieces as we walk through. Exiting the building on the other side onto a patio with seating scattered around it we walk through that to take a path nearly hidden by tall bushes. The path is lined in flowerbeds with identification markers throughout. The lighting is low and aimed more at the plants than anything else. The path forks at the entrance to a large glass greenhouse. He guides me over to it and opens a door for me. Inside I am transported to a tropical garden. It is warm and humid, but air circulates constantly, keeping it from being a sticky place. It is a wonderland of orchids and such. The scents are soft but enticing. As we walk through admiring the beauty of these plants I ask him, "Where are you from?"

"Originally? A castle in Ireland. It doesn't exist anymore. It was near a city that also no longer exists. Probably for the best."

"What was it like?"

"The city?" I nod yes and he continues, "It was old and hidebound. Everyone was supposed to behave this way during the day when all was lit and proper. At night, the upper class did as they pleased while the lower class tried to hide as best they could."

"Oh, sounds rough."

"I think it was for a great many. I didn't know it then. I was a child and did what I was taught was acceptable, believed everything I was taught to believe. Later when I became a vampire I spent a lot of time trying to figure out my place in things. I realized that much of what I had been taught was either unfinished or wrong. That vampire hearing will change your life, right?" He opens the door of the greenhouse and we exit to continue walking through the gardens outside.

"So, after you were turned and you started noticing things, what then?"

"I was still a very young man by the standards of the time. We weren't even to worry about getting married until we were near 30. So I started reading. I still appeared to party but I would find the most exhausted woman there and pretend I was really into her and we would go upstairs where I would explain to her I just wanted a quiet place to read without being bothered. Back then I was surprised by just how many women were happy about that. Now, not so much. That brought me to some friendships with these women and they eventually taught me things that made any woman I was with quite happy."

I laugh, "Yes, I can imagine." I turn to follow the scent of a flower and there is Mikael's shadow, he looks near mournful as he says, "Sebastian, how could you?"

Sebastian pushes me behind him and says, "You don't own her Mikael. She is her own person. What are you playing at?"

Mikael dissipates into smoke that disperses quickly. I step out from behind Sebastian and say, "You're sweet, but you don't have to put me behind you. That was a magical thing, I am better able to deal with it than you are."

He extends his arm, I take it and as we continue walking he says quietly, "I agree. But I would still protect you from danger as best I can every time, even if that is just standing between you and a thing while you prepare to blast it with your magic."

I hug his arm, "Thank you."

We walk in silence for time, as we near the main building again he says, "Have you fed tonight?"

"No, I've been busy. Why?"

"Want to go hunting with me?"

I grin, "You want me to go hunting with you?"

"I do. So what do you say?"

"Yes! Let's go! I haven't been hunting in a while."

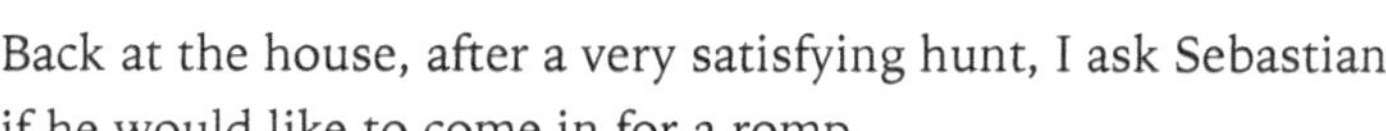

Back at the house, after a very satisfying hunt, I ask Sebastian if he would like to come in for a romp.

He asks, "Will I be staying with you until tomorrow night?"

I frown, "Well, I have an appointment I need to go to tomorrow, um, during the day. So you can but I will have to leave at some point."

"How? How are you going out during the day?"

"Shit. Come on, let's sit over here on the porch and I'll tell you a story." I tell him all about how I got this ability from Mikael and that Mikael tried turning me into the council for it but since I have a goddess backing me, I'm less worried about them now. I also let him know I just found out about a sunblock that will allow him to do this too. His eyes widen at that.

He chokes out, "You mean it is possible I could see the day again?"

"Oh shit, you really miss it don't you?"

"I do. I was a creature of the sunlight, the only reason I began going out at night was because that was when the parties were. I always made time to see the sunrise though. I would give anything…"

I see tears running down his face, staining his crisp white shirt and I do something stupid and impulsive, "Here." I tip my head and push my hair back from my shoulder on that side, "Drink. You don't have to drink much, just drink a little and I'll tell you why after."

He is confused but stands and walks over to me. He drops down to his knees, takes my face in his hands to kiss my lips gently. He moves one hand to cup my shoulder and presses his lips to my neck where it joins with my shoulder, I feel his mouth open and his fangs just touch my skin making me shiver. He sinks his teeth into me and I moan, he presses his nails into my shoulder as he drinks. My core clenches with need and I moan again. He withdraws, licking a drop from my neck. I realize my eyes are closed and I open them to see him sitting on his heels in front of me. "Now, tell me why I needed to drink from you."

"So you can see the sun. I— you wanted it so much and it was in my power to grant you that. And eventually you would find out that I have already passed it on before you. The first was Leonidas, we didn't know that I could pass it on that way. Then after I had an accident with some vines," he looks curious and I hold up a hand, "don't ask. I had to tell Scarlett and Chloe. They didn't really believe it but wanted to see just in case because they both wanted to be in the sunlight again. They spent the first day like cats curled up in the sunlight streaming through a window. It was sweet. Then the house was blown up and Eason was here. It was daytime and the choices were let him die or give him the ability too. So I did. And now you have it too."

Another tear rolls down his face, "You mean to tell me that when the sun comes up I will be able to stand in it and just enjoy the warmth on my face?"

"Yes. You will. You will also need to be careful. At least until I can meet with Nathan and swap the glamour spray for the sunblock recipe. Then you can just carry it with you and pretend that you are wearing that."

"What sunblock?"

"I just found out about it at the funeral. It's a whole thing. So, now that you will be free to go when you please, would you like to come inside for a romp or would you prefer to go home and wait for the sun to rise?"

"Mind if I come in, have a romp and wait for the sun here?"

"Not a bit. Let's go," I say with wide smile.

Jasmine

The day dawns bright and Sebastian is still sitting in the sunlight streaming through my bedroom window when I get out of the shower. It makes me a little sad that they have longed for the sun so much for so long and none of them even chose to be turned. I would give up a thousand sunrises for the freedom being a vampire has given me. I turn to my closet and step in to find some suitable clothes. I don't have the slightest idea what one wears to a reading of a will. After going through the hangers twice I decide they are getting me as I usually am. I dressed for his mother because though I knew her little I think very highly of her. My decision made I grab a pair of black jeans and slip them on, pairing them with a white button up and a black sweater, it is late in the year. I need to act like I am chilled even if I am nothing of the sort.

A quick stop in the bathroom for mascara and I walk across the room to kneel by Sebastian. "Hey, I have to go."

He blinks like he forgot where he was, "Oh, yes. I should go."

I put my hand on his arm as he starts to rise, "Don't worry about it. I think it might not be safe for others if you drive home right now. You are welcome to hang out here for as long as you need to. I have another lesson tonight, this time with Hekate. So I don't know when I'll be back. Enjoy the sun." I kiss his forehead as he settles in and then I head for the door and downstairs. I want to eat before I go. Scarlett and Chloe are in the kitchen when I get there, they've poured their bags into wine glasses. I check the time and decide to be fancy too. I lean in and give Scarlett a kiss as I grab a glass. Biting a hole in my bag I squeeze the blood into the glass and toss the bag in the trash. Taking a sip I ask, "So what are you two up to today?"

Chloe smiles, "I am going to curl up in my room and binge a show I've been missing. Eason is off on a business trip and I have been hunting a lot lately. I am ready to rest."

Scarlett laughs, "We have hunted a lot lately. I have plans for reading in the sun. It's a lounge day. What are you up to?"

"I am going out to a reading of a will. Oh, before I forget, Sebastian is upstairs sitting in the sun. I don't think he is going to move till it goes down but I am going to be out for at least the rest of the day. And, I have a sunblock deal happening that will mean you all have cover stories for going out during the day." I hear a ping on my phone and I pick it up to see it is Leonidas letting me know he is here, "I have to go, Leonidas just got here and he is my ride since it's his mom's will. We need a girls night to catch up." I walk over and give Scarlett another kiss before I rinse my cup and set it upside down in the sink. "Bye! Rest well my friends!"

I dash outside to Leonidas' truck and hop in. He pulls me close for a kiss, soft and sweet before releasing me and putting the truck in reverse. As he heads the truck toward the lawyer's office I ask him, "Has the lawyer given you any clue about why I need to be there?"

"I haven't talked to him since the funeral but no, no clue before that either. I was as surprised as you were. I guess we'll both find out shortly. The rest of the family is likely to be there and mad that you are there. Of course, I don't know who else is going to be there. My mother seems to have saved me some surprises for when she was gone." He smiles a sad kind of smile and I scoot closer so I can lean my head on his shoulder as my way of offering what comfort I can while he drives.

The lot at the lawyer's office is full so we have to park down the street a bit. As we walk up his paralegal comes out of the building and bustles over, one arm carting papers and the other a box, "Hi! Leonidas and Jasmine?" We nod and she turns on her heel, "Great! Follow me. This is the largest crowd we have ever had for a reading of a will. Your mother knew some folks! I think your entire family is here and boy are they mad as wet hens! Mr. Rinfell near threw the lot of them out once already. Once the others started showing up we moved over here to this conference room we rented as soon as we realized the number of people that would be here. They arrived two whole hours early and sat in the waiting room mad and mean! I told Mr. Rinfell they were here and he came out and reminded them of when it was scheduled for, invited them to go have lunch and come back. They weren't having it so he told them fine, sit in the waiting area, I have other things to do before then. I thought his head was going to blow clean off when the one said, 'We thought we could perhaps see the will early, get an idea of what it says. So we can be prepared.' I've never seen him that shade of red! Here we are, would you mind getting that door?" I step forward and pull one door open while Leonidas does the same for the other side, and we follow her in. She is quiet now as we walk into a conference room with a very long table. Along one side of the table his family sits facing us while the other side is filled with people from the funeral. Rinfell gestures toward two seats next to him on the side closest to us. His paralegal sets the box next to his foot and the papers near his hand. We sit in the chairs he indicated and he says, "Now we can get started."

I hear Tony mumble, "About fuckin' time." I contemplate draining him entirely later this evening but I have a feeling he would taste awful. He sneers at me and I reconsider as Rinfell clears his throat.

"We have a lot of small item bequeaths so I will go through the smaller items first. I will read off the item and call the person's name, they can sign for and collect their item and then return to their seat or leave as they choose." He goes on to go through so many items. The reading is just going on and on when I realize he hasn't said a single name in the family. Every single person that has come to collect an item has been part of the magical community. Things are suddenly more interesting as I begin to pay attention. As I watch I realize that each item glows briefly as it reaches its new owner. I set my hand on Leonidas's leg and whisper, "Can you see that?"

He watches a couple of the items and then shakes his head no. I meet eyes with the witch next to me and she grins. I wonder if it was her that spelled the items? As if she realizes what went through my head her grin grows wider and she tips her head in what seems an affirmation of my thought.

Every one of the people that has collected an item has returned to their seat and they are all watching expectantly. What am I missing? What is it that they know? The names drift into family names. Mostly they are bequeathed varying amounts of money and they all seem disgruntled by the amounts. Rinfell comes to Tony's name and says, "she left a message for you, would you rather it be read in private or would you prefer to hear it now in front of everyone?"

"Read it now and get on to what I get," he exclaims as his meaty fist pounds the table.

Rinfell smiles as he reads,

"Dearest Brother,

You were always a greedy bastard and I have left you a small sum of money. Not enough to pay for the schemes I know you will be using to attempt to take control of what was never yours to begin with. I go to my rest with the knowledge that you will be paying for your crimes very soon. I have seen how you will die and it gives me great satisfaction to know you will die in fear for your crimes against your own."

Tony jumps to his feet, Cheryl the paralegal watches him with an almost hungry look as he starts yelling, "That is defamation of character! Slander! I'll sue the shit out of the bitch for talking about that!"

Rinfell stands very slowly and a feeling of power flows through the room. Tony and the rest of the family can't feel it but all the magical folk get real still to see how this plays out. Rinfell watches as Tony falls silent. Rinfell speaks in a silky voice that feels like a knife to the throat, "Sir, you will keep yourself under control or I will have you taken away from here. Are we clear?"

Tony swallows, "Yes. I think we are. We are very clear."

Rinfell seats himself again, "Now, where was I? Oh yes, just after the note that made our friend here so angry. Tony is to receive a check in the amount of two thousand dollars."

Tony jumps up and starts yelling again, spittle flying. I watch Cheryl catch Rinfell's eye and he nods once at her. She near bounces over to Tony and takes one arm in her hand. Tony's eyes bulge as he draws a breath to scream at her. Then she starts walking and Tony is pulled inexorably along with her. He splutters and tries to pry her hand off his arm to no avail. The door shuts behind them and the room is silent for long moments.

Rinfell looks to the rest of the family still seated, "If you would prefer to join Tony outside with my associate, now is the time. If not, you will need to be extra quiet, no matter your opinion on the will."

They all sit very quietly as though afraid to even respond vocally. Rinfell watches them till he is satisfied and continues on, "Leonidas, you receive the balance of her monies and estates with one exception. Her home and everything contained within it beyond familial mementos goes to Jasmine."

"I'm sorry, please forgive me for interrupting you," I say as I lean forward, "but I thought I just heard you say that she left me her house?"

"You did. And I will explain further after the reading, if you can wait," he raises a brow and tips his head toward the only humans in the room. I cut my eyes toward them and each is listening intently.

I take a deep breath, "Yes. I can wait. I'm sorry, go on."

He smiles gently and says, "I understand. This is confusing. Now, Leonidas, your monies will arrive in a wire transfer and we will need to do some paperwork to retitle properties." Leonidas nods and Rinfell continues, "Now, that concludes the reading. All bequeathments have been dispersed or at least named. Everyone may leave with the exception of Jasmine and Leonidas as they have paperwork to finish." As he finishes speaking all of the magical community stand and start moving toward the door as it opens to admit Cheryl back into the room. Rinfell says, "Ah, excellent. Cheryl, I think some of our guests may need an escort from the building. Would you?"

Cheryl lights up and heads for the other side of the table as the family all stand up right then and move quickly toward the door by going the long way around the table so as to avoid contact with Cheryl. For her part, Cheryl stops next to the box she had been standing by before she escorted Tony from the room. Her eyes follow them as they push past everyone else to exit the room.

She meets my eyes when they are gone and winks at me. I think we could be really good friends and I smile at her. Rinfell clears his throat as he glances between the two of us with a raised brow, "Cheryl, the documents for Mr. Knight please."

She passes a stack over to Leonidas and shows him the label system of where to sign and where to initial for each of them. Rinfell looks to me, "Jasmine, may I call you Jasmine?" At my nod he continues, "You have inherited Alena's home. The one she spent most of her adult life in. She asked that I explain to you that a great many spaces in that house are not what they seem and that you should be cautious until you learn more. There are keys to some and for others you are the key. You will need to speak with Father Neally, he has some information that she didn't trust me with. She saw so many things, it is likely she did me a service in having Father Neally keep certain things. I digress. Here are keys to your home. It has been in your name for years at this point, so no paperwork for you. There will be the matter of getting the smell of dog out once Leonidas's associates leave."

"Oh, I don't mind the smell of dog."

"Well, that will make it easier for you. Now, you will need to place the palm of your hand on the number plate next to the door before you go in. Hold it there until you hear the chime. She said it is very important that you do that. Said it would key the house to your energy and wake it up, help it remember you." My jaw drops at that and he holds up a hand, "I don't know what she means by remember you. She said a great many things that didn't make sense then and still don't now, yet I am one of the long-lived races. You would think that at least would help me to figure out some of her more cryptic remarks. It really has not." He chuckles, "She is the reason I work as a lawyer. She told me it would be how I meet my mate. I haven't yet, but I am continuing to work as a lawyer because I have that much belief in her predictions. They always come to pass. Though I am told you broke a prophecy. That is no matter, Alena never thought the prophecy would be what happened. She said you would change things in ways they never imagined. Ah, Leonidas is finished. One other thing, her house is protected. Heavily. Considering the events happening in your life, I think it may be prudent for you to get yourself living in the house as soon as possible. Perhaps gather some clothing and begin staying there tonight."

"How do you know about events in my life?" He just raises a brow and realization dawns on me, "Oh. Yes. Well. I might go stay there tonight. Thank you."

Eleven

Jasmine

Leonidas looks over at me as he drives out of the parking lot, "Ready to see your new place?"

"I don't know? Are you ok with this? Don't you want your mom's house? You could have it. I would give it back to you."

"No. I just inherited multiple properties that I now have to deal with, you are not adding this one to them. I am really fine with you having her place. Besides," he slants a look over at me, "you having it means I have great reasons for visiting as often as I like. And I get to make new happy memories in the house I grew up in. It's a win for me. All the fun and none of the responsibility."

"I guess when you put it that way, yes. Take me to see the house. I don't know what I am going to do with it still. I mean, you just rebuilt our house and we had it decorated, it is perfect. I love our house. I don't know how I could leave it."

The drive is short and we arrive. The house is old, Victorian style. It looks lonely, as weird as that sounds. Banner and two others from Leonidas's wolf crew step out the front door and walk out to the truck to talk. I leave them talking to Leonidas about how much longer they need to stay here and I head for the house. I step up on the porch and I feel a tingle. It reminds me of what Rinfell said about putting my hand somewhere before I go in. I look around the door for a likely place and I am coming up with nothing. I see a doorbell, an old bell with a chain, and a number… that's it! The number plate! I place my hand on the number plate and I wait, feeling incredibly silly. I can hear their conversation as a faint buzz as I wait and I hope they aren't paying attention to this. I hear a chime sound from everywhere and nowhere. That must be the sign.

Taking my hand from the number plate I open the screen door and walk in, a feeling washes over me and I stop where I stand. Tears start flowing as I wrap my arms around myself, I am home. I haven't felt like I was home since ever but this place, this place is home. This is the place I longed for always. Every time my aunt sent another client, every time Fabio hit me, when Mikael tried to kill me; this is where I wanted to go and I never knew. I never knew home was a real place. I thought it was just something I wished for, a place that felt like I belonged. I hear the door open behind me and a pair of hands spin me around to face Leonidas as he inspects me for damage, "Jasmine, are you all right? What happened? Talk to me!"

I sniffle and straighten myself to tell him, "I'm home." More tears flow as Leonidas moves from concern to puzzled, "I walked in and I was home. I've never been home before. Never been in a place that I remember that felt like home. The feeling of coming home was so foreign that it broke my heart a little to finally feel it." I look at him through eyes blurred with blood tears, "Leonidas, I don't ever want to live anywhere else again."

He smiles softly and takes me in his arms, "And you don't have to. This is your house. We'll get your things and you can come straight back here and soak it up. But first, let's dry your tears so you can see the rest of the house properly."

He walks me through the house with the guys following behind. It is mostly decorated in old things and I love it. The style is eclectic and charming in the best way. We get back to the front door and I turn to look at Banner, "I know you all are ready to get home but can you wait long enough for me to get my things and get back?"

He smiles at me, "We can, for the price of a hug. You look like you could use one or three and what do you know, there's three of us here."

A watery chuckle escapes my lips as I walk over and hug them one at a time, finishing with Banner. He whispers, "You call if you need us. For anything."

I struggle not to cry again as I nod and exit the house.

Leonidas drops me off at the house and leaves for his job site as I am heading in on my mission to get back home as fast as possible. It occurs to me that the house may have been spelled to make me feel this way. I shrug it off though, unless the house plans to eat me as sacrifice to bring her back I am fine with it. Hell, there isn't much I would balk at doing for the feeling of being home. Leonidas held me close to him the whole ride back to the house and it helped but now he is off to work and I just want to go home.

As I take the stairs two at a time I shout for Scarlett and Chloe. If they aren't here I will call them when I get home. In my room I grab the duffel from the top shelf and unzip it so I can toss my clothes in. Scarlett and Chloe walk in as I snatch things off hangers and stuff them in the bag. I look up and smile, "She left me a house. And I am going to go live there. You can both come if you want, but I have to go. I have to be there."

I keep shoving clothes into the bag until Scarlett grabs my hands, "Jasmine! Slow down, what are you talking about? You're scaring us."

I stop trying to finish packing and really look at them. Chloe is wringing her hands and her lips are pressed into a thin line. Scarlett has hold of both my hands and her eyes are wide, her breathing faster than it should be. "I'm sorry, I didn't mean to scare you. Leonidas's mother left me her house in her will. I went to see it and it feels like the home I have always longed for, up till now the closest I have come to that feeling was the trailer that I got when I left Mikael's and that was more about it being my space than it feeling like a home. This place, I walked in and I was home."

Chloe nods, "I always felt that way in my mother's house. I have never understood the magic that makes this place a home and not that place, but if you found a place that feels like home, I don't blame you. I would probably go stay there for a few decades or so because it would take that long to pry me out of the place."

Scarlet releases my hands, "It feels like home? So much that you are willing to leave the house that we all just had rebuilt and then decorated to suit us?"

I look in her eyes, "Yes."

She nods her head a few times, "Ok. Then I guess I need to go pack."

Chloe puts an arm out to stop Scarlett leaving, "Wait. I want to talk to you both." Scarlett backs up and shoves her thumbs in her pockets, "Well, Eason and I have been talking about moving in together, but we didn't want to cramp the bachelor pad lives we have going in both our houses so we were going to find a new place. But, if you are both moving out, would you mind it terribly if I just let him move in? I know it is against what we talked about, but I think we assumed that we would all be living here and… well… what do you think?"

I look at Scarlett and we both smile big and dive over at Chloe to crush her doubts with hugs. I tell her, "Of course I don't mind! You are both the sweetest together. Move him in and you have all my blessings."

Scarlett laughs, "You have all of our blessings, I completely agree with Jasmine. Move your Eason in and the two of you enjoy knocking around in this place. Now, if you don't mind, I am off to pack. I have to catch up, Jasmine is going to leave without me."

We laugh as she extracts herself from our group hug. I give Chloe one more squeeze and tell her, "I am so happy for you. I wish you every happiness possible."

She squeezes me back and we release each other. She wipes her eyes and her voice only a little watery says, "I need to go call Eason and give him the news. I'll be coming to see your new place really soon."

She turns and near runs out of my room as I go back to my packing. Very quickly I have my huge duffle and a large suitcase packed with pretty much everything from my room that I need. The rest can stay here, it's all decorative or books I have already read. Leaving them here means I have plenty of space for getting new books. I shut my bedroom door as I walk out with bags in tow. Scarlett meets me at the top of the stairs, carrying her own luggage. We get to the driveway and she asks, "Is there space for more than one car?"

"Yes. The driveway there is actually longer than what we have here."

"Great. I'll follow you."

I am grinning as I toss my bags in the back and get in the driver seat of my car. Pulling out of the driveway I finally head home.

The trip home is quick and I am so happy to be back. Banner is the only one still here, he walks out to meet me at my car as I get out. "Hello beautiful. Your home is waiting for you." He insists on carrying one of my bags, even after I point out that I could throw him if I wanted. "Let me be nice to you

Jasmine. I don't care that you are strong like bear, I want to be nice to you."

"Um, ok. Thank you. Are you going to carry one of Scarlett's too?" I ask as she pulls in behind me.

He grins, "Yes, but only because it pisses her off when I am nice to her."

"What? Why?"

He says over his shoulder as he heads for Scarlett and her bags, "It's a long story. Maybe I'll tell you one day."

I watch as Scarlett gives him a look that could freeze lava and then tosses one of her bags at his head. He laughs as he catches it and starts up the drive toward me and the house.

Scarlett turns and catches sight of me, "You didn't tell me you got a dog Jasmine."

Banner laughs so hard he nearly drops her bag. I can't help but laugh as we walk in with Scarlett trailing behind. She shoves past him as she walks in the house. Stopping in the middle of the room she says, "This place does feel good. I'm going to find myself a room. Tell me you are going to put the damn dog out before I come back down."

I laugh, "Don't worry, Banner is going to leave." I hear her grumbles as she walks off still carrying the one bag.

Banner is still chuckling as he sets our bags down on a couch. He hefts his own bag from beside the couch and says to me, "The short story is that I played a prank and got her good and she has never forgiven me. It was too easy though and nothing was damaged."

Shaking my head at him I hold the door for him as he walks through, "How long has she been holding the grudge?"

He turns and grins, "Only ten years or so…"

"Really? Ten years?"

"Yeah. She was embarrassed that she had been got. It's fine. She'll get over it one day. How about this, you come to lunch with me and I'll spill all the sordid details."

"Or I could just ask her?"

"Ah, you could. But then you would miss out on the joys of lunch with me."

"I mean, lunch sounds nice and all except for one thing."

"What's that?"

"Well, I'm a vampire. It kind of limits my diet, you know?"

He sighs like I'm a dunce, "I can smell what you are, did you think I wouldn't take you to a place that would provide the right food for you?"

My brows scrunch, "There are places that do that?"

"Of course. Leonidas hasn't taken you to any?"

"No?"

He shrugs, "Maybe he doesn't know. So you should come out to lunch with me and then you can take him there some other time."

I tip my head to one side as I think, "Um, ok. Yes. I think that might be fun. And besides, it isn't like you smell bad or something."

He lifts his head and sniffs the air, "You definitely don't smell bad. Maybe you could wear a red hood and we'll talk about how long my tongue is before I eat you."

His voice goes gravely as he says that and my panties get wet as a shiver works its way through my body. He inhales deeply and growls, his eyes flash as he looks at me.

"Sir, Imma need you to go on about your business. We'll talk about hoods and eating later. Have a good day at work."

He growls again, "I'll message you about that date." Then he blows me a kiss before turning to walk to his car.

I shut the door and lean against it for a moment, eyes closed to calm my raging hormones and nearly jump out of my skin when Scarlett says, "Ugh. I suppose you could do worse than a jackass wolf." She laughs as I try to breath again.

"That was shady ma'am. Funny, but shady. What do you have against him anyway?"

"He plays too much."

"Mmhmm." I say with a raised brow as I cross my arms in front of my chest. "Care to explain?"

"No. I do not. I am sure he will. And I won't be mad about that." She sighs as she picks up her bag, "If I am honest, I'm not really mad anymore. I just like to let him think I am. It keeps him from pranking me again and makes other people think twice about it."

I laugh, "Well, I guess I understand that. Don't worry, I won't tell him that you aren't really mad at him anymore."

She says, "I left you the master bedroom. Have you been in there yet?"

I grab my bags and follow her, "No, I haven't. Why?"

"There is a note for you. The writing on it looks feminine. Like his mom left it? But, that's not possible, right? I mean, she didn't meet you till you got with Leo, right?"

"Um, no she didn't. But she was a very powerful psychic or seer, whatever you call them. She might have left it before she went into the nursing home."

Now I need to get my ass to the master bedroom and read that note. Scarlett left the door open for me and I am grateful. I stop in the doorway to take in the room. It is dark. And there are protection amulets up on each of the walls. I have seen them throughout the house too, now that I think about it. What on earth could cause her to need so much protection? The bed is gorgeous. Old, solid, dark wood four post bed with curtains tied back to each post. There are two dressers and a vanity, all in dark wood to match the bed frame. I set my bags down next to the door as I spot an envelope on the vanity. Crossing the room and seating myself, I pick up the envelope. It has a thick layer of dust on it, my name can still be clearly read. Using my magic I open a window and send a little breeze over it to take all the dust and carry it outside, closing the window as the last of it flows out. A single piece of tape holds it closed and I slip a finger under it to lift gently.

The paper is scented, it smells like her. I unfold it and start to read,

My darling Jasmine,

.   .   .

I hope we met before I left this plane of existence. This will all make so much more sense if you at least met me, but I can't see that. It's too close to my own death. If not, well, I hope you at least found my son. He is a good person, even when most won't see it that way. He thinks I don't know he is a vampire but I knew before he was turned that it would happen.

This house is special and unfortunately, I must leave most of the explanations why to others that will be here in person. I have seen much of what you went through in dreams and visions, so while you don't know me I feel like I know you very well. You should know, you are stronger than you think. You are more capable than you believe. You will achieve anything you set your mind to doing.

Trust in the ones your heart and your intuition choose, they will always have your back. And listen when they tell you someone is bad. They are never wrong. As well you know. Love. Love as many as it takes and know that they will love you back exactly as you are.

I wish with all my heart that we had time to be friends, just know that I love you so much. I'm sorry I had to thrust all this on you like this. But I know you can do it.

Love,

Alena

Twelve

Jasmine

Alena's note left me unsettled. I feel like my home is coming with strings attached. I won't leave my home, so I need to get things figured out. But I won't be able to stop thinking about it if I don't work at finding out what it is so I call the priest.

His phone rings twice and he answers, "Father Neally, how can I help you?"

"Hello. This is Jasmine—"

"Jasmine! I have been waiting for your call. I was beginning to wonder if I would have to track you down myself."

"Sorry, I have been really busy. Did you know about the house?"

"I did. I do. I know more than you do at this point. When can you meet with me?"

"Are you free in an hour or two? I was going to head to a bookstore. I need to learn some things."

"Perfect. I am at the cathedral, doing some paperwork. Bane of my life. I will be here the rest of the day. You stop by and come on in the front doors, they chime in my office when they are opened, I'll come out and collect you."

"Thank you Father Neally, I'll see you soon."

Ending that call I search out one of the other cards I was given the day of the funeral. Caden's card falls into my hand like magic and I am too grateful to be bothered by it. I dial before I lose my nerve. Caden answers before the first ring finishes, "Jasmine, I am so glad you called."

I look at my phone like it will provide answers before I say, "How did you know it was me?"

"The only other people that call this number are already listed in my phone. When no name popped up I knew it must be you."

"Oh. That is really reasonable. So, um, you wanted to meet with me?"

"Yes. We do. Would tonight be a convenient time for you?"

"Yes, yes. It would. I am at Alena's place, I moved in last night. Can I ask you something?"

"Please do."

"What does it feel like to you? When you walk into Alena's house?"

"That isn't the question I expected. You are full of surprises. It feels comfortable. Inviting. Friendly. May I ask why you want to know?"

"Um, yes. When I got here, it felt like the home I had never had. It is amazing and a little frightening now that I have had time to think about it."

He chuckles, "Fair enough. I can help you with that. She said the place had always been waiting for you. It tolerated her but it was always waiting for you. I don't know how she knew that, perhaps one of the witches could fill you in. Lacey perhaps, she was good friends with Alena, beyond our work together. I look forward to seeing you tonight. Ten good for you?"

I agree to ten and we end the call. I feel a great sense of relief having made those two calls.

Only one more call to make, Nathan. This one doesn't bother me at all. He is thrilled to hear from me, especially when he finds out I have several bottles and a spell for him. He agrees to meet me at the book store parking lot for the trade.

Now, on to the book store.

I have been through the shelves of Helen's bookstore so many times, right now I am waiting for them to get new books and I found another bookstore that only operates during the day. I gave Nathan the address to this place, he was waiting when I pulled up. We swapped out recipes and I gave him the spray bottles I had already created. He did a dance in the parking lot and then said he had to run, there were some vampires hoping to get this before the funeral of their friends and he wanted to make it happen. I wished him well and told him I was at Alena's place if he needed more and couldn't get another to do it. He saluted me as he peeled out of the parking lot.

Heart full, I head into the book store.

Hake

I am browsing the shelves when I see her walk in. She is so much more a vision than the surveillance pictures Mikael has up in his house. I see now why he is so determined to possess her. The light of her would lift up any man that held her as his. What a prize. Abandoning the magazines I had been perusing I work my way around the book store to be near her. I can feel the magic in her, even this far away. She is powerful. Does she know? Why wouldn't she hide it?

I am glad I keep my power hidden as a matter of course, best if she thinks I am human. I look at the books she is picking up, eco-investing? What is she doing with that? As if she is going to be able to handle investing. That's a man's world. I shadow her as she moves on to the hippie section. All that recycle bullshit. She has five books in her arms already when she moves into the home renovation section. That's my in.

I stroll over and browse near her without getting close enough to set off any alarms. Picking up a thick book on house remodeling I flip through the pages. Keeping an eye on her I see her moving through the books and I put the one

I have back just in time to reach for the same one as her. Our hands touch, her hands are soft and cool, I jerk back and say, "Oh! I'm sorry," with the most charming smile I can conjure.

She smiles back and says, "Go ahead, it looks like there is another copy here."

"Are you renovating a house?"

She looks up from the book, "Mmm, thinking about it. But mostly I want to learn about taking care of an older house."

"Nice! I haven't seen many women working at that. Old houses are so rewarding though, I just love them. Have you lived in it long?" I can't get a good read on her. She has that buzz of power around her and it blurs everything. I can't tell if she is falling for this shit or not!

"Not long, no. Have you worked on many?"

"Yes, it is a passion of mine. I buy them and live in them while I restore them, selling them when I am ready to move on to the next project."

"That sounds lovely. And it provides gorgeous homes for people too."

"It does. Say, would you like to get together sometime soon? I could offer you some tips and tricks for caring for your home, if you would be interested in that?"

She eyes me and I do my best to project innocence. Finally she says, "I would like to know more about caring for my old house."

"Great. If you'll give me your number I'll call you after I have the chance to check my schedule," I make the alarm on my phone go off at that moment, "oh, I need to get going. I have an appointment with a plumber."

She is eyeing me as I smile kindly, but she pulls paper and pen from her purse and writes down a number. "Here you go, I would like to talk with you about old houses."

She emphasizes old houses and I worry she isn't quite falling for my act. I thank her and exit quickly, telling her I will call soon. I feel her eyes on me as I leave the bookstore so I quickly walk out of view of the windows. I'll bide my time. When I call her I will be much more knowledgeable about old houses. Thankful I had the foresight to park around back I hurry to my car. It wouldn't do for her to see me still out here when she leaves the book store.

Jasmine

I leave the book store with only eight books and I think I did well. Father Neally's cathedral isn't far from the house and happily, the traffic from the book store is light. I park close to the door as the parking lot has no vehicles in it today. I can see the rectory behind the cathedral, it looks like a nice place. Walking up the steps to the cathedral is weird. I haven't gone to services of any sort since my aunt started trying to sell me to the parishioners at her church. Walking in here alone is not the most comfortable thing, but I hold to the fact that Alena trusted Father Neally. With her history there is no way she would trust someone that didn't deserve her trust. Pushing the door open I step into the dim building. The lights are off because there are no services happening right now but the stained glass windows are huge and they cast multi-colored bands of light across the room.

I am a dozen or so pews in when Father Neally comes through a curtain and says, "Jasmine! I'm so glad you are here! Come, come, back here."

I follow him through a curtained door and down a short hall into a large office. It has various chairs and no couch. My shoulders release seeing that and I realize that being alone in a strange place with a man I barely know was freaking me out and something as simple as the fact that he has no couch in his office helped me to relax. I need therapy.

He seats himself behind his desk and I sit in a chair across from him. He opens a drawer in front of him, shuffles his hand around in it a bit and then I hear a click. He grins and reaches down and off to the side, his hand coming back up with a key clutched in it. He shuts the drawer he dug around in and another click sounds. Setting the key on the desk in front of him he says, "This is it. This is the key that is going to change your life. This key goes to a door that is in the house. You will never see the door unless you intend to find it." He looks up at me with a sparkle in his eye, "I bet you would like for me to get to the point of things now, eh?" I nod firmly and he laughs, "You are in luck. Alena didn't just leave you a house. She left you a job too. She deeply wished that she would be the one to tell you about the job but she knew that wouldn't be happening. So she left at least part of it to me. Have you heard of the Library of Alexandria? The Great Library?"

I tip my head to one side as my brows draw down, "Yes. It was burnt to the ground a long time ago. Readers are still mad."

"What if I told you it never happened? The burning of the library that is. At least, not the collection that was housed inside anyway."

"Well, that doesn't make sense. How would they — Why— I need more information please."

"Well, knowledge was and is power. The Ptolemy line of rulers had amassed a vast collection of books, because they were collectors. The whole family loved to read and collect books. They did not discriminate in any way and they had the money and power to obtain copies or originals of many books of power. Eventually as people realized what was contained in that building they tried to steal tomes, take over the building, or the entire kingdom. It just became unsafe for it to be so visible. Ptolemy I Soter charged Demetrius of Phaleron with founding the library. Demetrius was the one that went to the Ptolemy III with the idea that the library needed to go into hiding. He had heard whispers of more attacks coming and he was at that time, quite old. He was also human. So, together they found a group of people that would be able to hide the library in time and space to preserve the tomes within forever. Do you see what I am getting at?"

"You have got to be joking. They didn't."

"They did. And it has been the best kept secret ever since. There are guardians, Alena being the first human guardian ever. It is still rumored and some manage to track it down. Which is why we still have guardians, even now. There was an attack not too long ago, but it was successfully repelled before they got in the building. Alena was more librarian and less guardian, meaning that she didn't do much fighting, however, she was recruited because of her skills as a seer. She prevented so many attacks. But, she has been the only one of her kind ever. You would be librarian and guardian because you are most definitely a scrapper."

"A what?"

"Scrapper, fighter, someone that can fight the things that go bump in the night like us. Shifters, witches, vampires, and various other creatures."

"Oh. I see. So I would be a librarian and a guardian, if I choose to accept this?"

He laughs, "If. Yes, you will be a guardian librarian. I don't even know you that well but I know you won't walk away from the opportunity to serve in your own way. But, I suppose I should ask, Jasmine, will you take up the key?"

I bite my lip. This is a lot of responsibility. I don't know if I can do this. Wait, it wouldn't be just me, he said group of people. Maybe I can do this? I would have access to a whole library, the greatest library the world has ever seen. Fuck it, if need be I will die trying. Extending my hand palm up I say, "Yes, I will take the key."

He laughs and scoops the key up to drop it in my hand, "I figured if nothing else the books would lure you. Only readers sound so salty when they talk about the library being burned to the ground."

I laugh too, because this guy has read me like a book. "Well, you aren't wrong. In fact, you seem very good at reading people. Is that a talent or something you learned?"

His smile fades, "When I was a young shifter I wanted more than anything to be a spiritual leader. I feel a deep connection to my deities and I want to do good things with that.

Becoming a priest at a young age in an organization riddled with power hungry monsters leaves you open for a great many things. I learned quickly from my fellow priests who in the organization should be trusted and from my parishioners I learned even more. It is learned. Mostly the hard way and if I am reading you right, the hard way is how you learned to scan places unfamiliar to you and to watch for red flags and means of escape."

I look away because he isn't wrong and I feel a little laid bare. "You read correctly."

He shifts in his chair, "I am sorry the world is not kind yet. I can promise you that you need never fear me and if you ever need help, I am a call away."

I meet his eyes again to see a deep sadness within them, "Thank you. I appreciate that."

He nods, "I am also here if you need a friend. Or someone to talk books. I am a frequent patron of the library you guard. Others will explain more to you about how it works. For now, I think we covered the important things. How are you holding up? I can imagine this is a lot."

I chuckle, "My normal has been a lot for some time, I am not sure when that will change. Being chosen for a prophecy is not all it's cracked up to be. Especially if you then go and break the entire prophecy so you guide book is now trash."

He laughs loudly at that, "Alena said she didn't see the prophecy being fulfilled or unfulfilled and it puzzled her for quite some time. I like to think that wherever she is she had a good laugh when she figured out that you broke the whole damn thing."

Thirteen

Jasmine

I make it home with a little time to spare before Caden and the others are supposed to show up so I grab a glass of blooded wine and sit down with the books I got today for an initial flip through. I know I won't have time to get into any one of them but I can leaf through them while I wait. The key feels like it is burning a hole in my pocket and my focus. I want to go explore it but I have a feeling I would be in there for way too long.

I hear steps on the porch, a glance at the window tells me Caden and the others have arrived. I am relieved to some extent as I cross the room to open the door for them. "Welcome to the house. I don't quite know what to call it just yet. Please, come in and ignore my awkward greeting."

They file in, Caden chuckling through introductions while two others scowl and the elf appears to be reserving judgement. Closing the door I ask them if they would like refreshments, Caden says, "Yes please." The witch and wolf decline, but the elf requests a glass of wine.

I excuse myself to the kitchen while mentally cursing my lack of foresight. Thank the gods I am a witch. I call in a bottle of a sweet Riesling and pour that for the elf, while Caden gets some of what I am having. I bring them out on a tray, handing each their glass before I set the tray on the coffee table and take my seat again. "So, you all wanted to talk to me?"

Caden finishes sipping his blooded wine with his eyes closed in enjoyment, "Yes. We do. First, have you met with Father Neally yet?"

"I have. Really nice man."

"Good. That makes this all so much easier. We are the other guardians in this area. Your crew, your backup as it were. This area was quickly seen as a weaker link area because those that try to steal from the library or take it as their own took Alena at face value. They discounted entirely that she was a seer and had no idea that she was an amazing strategist. Her ability to see a thing coming and act to counter it in the best way possible was nothing short of stunning. She made our work much easier. We know precious little about you, for all that she spoke of you often. Tell me, what are you gifted with?"

"Well, first, I got this mouth. It runs with the best of them and I will hurt some feelings. Second, like you, I am vampire. So I have better strength than many. My not so secret weapon is that I am also a witch. My very secret weapon is that I don't need the sunblock."

Caden's jaw drops open to hang until the elf stretches her arm over to close it. He immediately opens it again and says, "What? How? How is that possible?"

"It's a long story. The short and only sort of accurate version is that it is a perk for being the chosen one."

Lacey rolls her eyes, "And the longer version?"

Raising a brow at her I say, "Is a tale for another day. That is why I gifted you the short version."

She gasps as though I stabbed her, Caden says, "Stop being so damn dramatic Lacey. Just because she is witch and vampire doesn't make her a threat to your position. Your theatrics are tiresome. Jasmine, I am sure you will understand why I say, you know this has to be kept secret from everyone? Including your family or friends or lovers."

"No." I shake my head emphatically, "absolutely not. I will not keep secrets from those I consider family. Under no circumstances will I put them in danger by association and leave them unaware. What the hell kind of person are you trying to make me into?"

Nia leans forward, "Explain." When Caden tries to cut me off she waves a hand at him and he is silenced, his face twisting in rage.

"Secrets in a family are a recipe for abuse and mistrust. How could I expect them to trust me if I can't even tell them the truth of what danger they are in for associating with me?" I look at each of them in turn as I continue, "None of you can honestly say that the ones after the library would never stoop to harming the ones I love to attempt to gain control of the library. And without a one hundred percent certainty that they would be safe, I will not hide the dangers from them. That you would even ask it of anyone is fucked up and makes me wonder about you as people. Can I even trust you to have my back if you would do that to the ones you love?"

Nia nods and waves at Caden, releasing him. He snarls at her, "You do that again and I will bite you."

She smiles a cold smile, "Promises, promises." Looking to me she says, "You are the first to demand this. And the only one to ever have reasoned it out so well. I like you. You have shown more thought in your words than this lot has in a very long time. I will tell you my secret. My loved ones know. I made no promises and only said that I understood why they would ask that. You tell your loved ones and you take responsibility, as I have, for ensuring that none of them lets your secrets fly."

Nia leans back in her seat, sipping her Riesling with a small smile. Looking around the room I see why she is smiling, the other three are stunned. Mouths gaping open like fish out of water. I bite the inside of my cheek to stop myself from grinning and quickly sip my blooded wine.

Caden is the first to recover and he downs the rest of his blooded wine before speaking, "How could you keep this from us Nia?"

Nia raises a brow, "Alena knew and the evidence was there. I didn't hide it. You saw and believed as you would. If you had asked if I would keep it secret I would have told you no. You didn't ask that. You asked for understanding of why you would request the secrecy. Same as you did with Jasmine now. Her mouth would have many in the elven court hating her. Her salvation would be that she is so very powerful. I think she may rival the king even. I don't know if he would like that or hate it. Probably best to stay out of his lands either way. He is kind of a prick."

Caden puts a hand to his forehead and massages it as he sighs. "Elves. Women. The whole fucking lot. What the hell am I going to do with this?"

I can't decide if I am offended by his generalization or entertained. Possibly some of both. "If I understood you correctly, you are backup, correct?"

Caden eyes me, his face tight, "Yes. Why?"

"Well, back up in general means not the person calling the shots. Alena was the guardian and she left it to me to take up her space. Wouldn't that put me in charge?"

Nia grins, "Maybe you wouldn't do so poorly in court."

Frank speaks up, "I don't give a ruddy damn who thinks they're in charge. The fucking library stays secret or--"

This time I wave a hand and silence Frank by freezing his vocal cords temporarily. He tries to stand as he appears to be snarling at me but I simply wrap him in bands of air. I feel a whisper of magic from Lacey and I pop a reflective bubble around her so that anything she attempts to send out will return directly to her. She is quickly very uncomfortable as she apparently tried to send something that falls like rain and burns like acid at me. So very rude. I hear laughter and turn to see Nia has lost all her composure and is laughing hard at Lacey. I think I could really get along with Nia. Caden is sitting very still and watching the other two.

Lacey appears to be tending to herself so I focus on Frank for the moment, "Are you quite finished trying to prove your power?"

Eyes cast down Frank nods and I release his vocal cords and his body. He clears his throat, "Sorry about that. I think maybe I got carried away. Alena was a very agreeable sort and I think maybe we all got the idea that we were actually in charge as she had such a gentle touch."

"I understand. Do we all understand that I am not Alena nor do I have a gentle touch?"

Caden nods, "I think we maybe get the point. Lacey appears ready to come out as well."

I release Lacey carefully, waiting to see if she thinks she is sneaky. Not even a whisper of magic flows out. Eyeing her I wait to see if she will apologize or not. She attempts to look down her nose at me but fails and says, "Oh fine! I apologize! I shouldn't have cast at you."

Hm, I take notice that she doesn't mention not doing it again and I nod, my lips pressed together. She will need watching. I stand, "Well, I feel like that is really all the talking or insult I will take in my own home for the rest of the day at the least. As lovely as it was talking to all of you, you really must go."

Caden nods as he stands and the others do as well, Nia finishing her Riesling as she does. Caden moves to the door, the wolf and the witch following. Nia dawdles and I feel like she wants to speak to me so I walk ahead to ensure the others leave.

The wolf and the witch are walking away by the time I get to the door. Caden is standing on the porch, he turns as I come to the door. "I wanted to apologize. We were rude. I hope you will still be willing to work with us after our poor behavior."

I nod, "I will give you three a second chance but I won't be turning my back on any of you any time soon. Goodbye Caden."

I shut the screen door and turn to Nia, hovering in the doorway to the living space we were all in. She watches Caden walk away and she whispers, "Lacey left you a nasty surprise in her chair."

I raise my brows and walk over to look at the chair. I don't see anything at first, I refocus my eyes and there, in the crevice toward the back of the chair is a little strand of magic. It has the slightest red glow to it. Anyone not looking for it would miss it. Sneaky indeed. I pop a bubble over the chair to contain any fallout, just like the one at the book store training room. Reaching in with my magic I trigger the spell. We both jump as the chair explodes. The bubble is filled with smoke and as we wait for it to clear, I hear my Scarlett pull into the drive. She walks into the house and sees us watching the bubble from the doorway. She steps up behind us, "Jasmine, why is there a bubble where a chair was and why are we watching the bubble?"

I shrug, "One of my co-workers doesn't like me at all. She left a trap." I gesture between Nia and Scarlett, "Nia, Scarlett; Scarlett, Nia. Nia is not the coworker that left the trap. Scarlett is one of my lovers, she is going to know all about this and she lives here with me."

They exchange greetings and the smoke settles enough that we can see the splinters and shreds that make up the remains of the chair. Scarlett asks, "What the hell did you do to your coworker to make her not like you that much?"

Nia and I turn to look at Scarlett, "I refused to keep my job a secret from you all because of the danger it will put you in."

She looks past us at the wreckage, "If your coworkers are that mean what the hell kind of people are you going to be fighting?"

Hake

Mikael has summoned me to answer to him. He thinks every thing will move at a lightening pace because he wills it so. I don't know what exactly he thinks I will have accomplished in the little time I have had. Pulling up to the manor I park and cut the engine. I'm still sitting there when that creepy fuck Vigo appears next to my door. He makes it very tempting to refuse to come here in the evenings at all.

I let him escort me into the house and to the study Mikael spends most of his time in. The man is locked in the past. He thinks the world is still the same as it was a few hundred years ago and it just isn't true. Vigo gestures for me to sit in a chair across from Mikael in front of the fire as he pour drinks for us both. Mikael would be properly horrified if he knew how much I hate his brandy. Vigo hands our drinks to us and leaves the room.

Mikael takes a sip and asks, "What do you have to report?"

I turn my glass in my hands, "Precious little. She has moved again. I am not sure where just yet, her habits are suddenly changed."

"She must know you are tracking her. Or perhaps she is spooked by the shades you have sent at her."

"Possibly. Either way, it will take more time for me to have a substantial report for you."

"Hmmph. I expect to hear from you within the next week. The longer this goes on the better her chances of slipping out of my grasp and we cannot have that. Our world depends on it."

"Well, then I should get back to it. No need to have Vigo escort me, I can find the way out myself." He nods as I set my brandy down on the table untouched and leave. Following the route Vigo has led me on every time I left the manor. Back in my car I hurry to start it and get rolling down the drive before they can think of a reason to stop me.

Jasmine

The kitchen in this house is old and well used. I love it. The appliances are antique and still work perfectly. I don't eat anymore but I miss the smell of baking things. The homey feel of a kitchen with someone cooking in it. Maybe I could bake things and give them away. Or maybe I am just feeling unsettled and want some comfort after Lacey tried to explode my living room because I wouldn't take her shit.

My phone rings and I answer it without looking, "Hello."

"Hi, is this Jasmine? This is Hake from the book store."

"Oh, hello Hake. How are you?"

"I am well. I am calling to ask if you would like to meet me for coffee and books tomorrow? If you are free?"

"Um," I go over what I have planned and I can't think of anything important or time consuming happening tomorrow, "sure. I have an hour or so that I could spare to talk books."

"Wonderful! There is a cafe just down the strip from the book store we met at, will that work for you or is it too far for you?"

What an odd way to put that. "It's fine, it's not like I'm walking. What time?"

"Say around one?"

"Perfect. I'll see you then Hake. Bye." Hitting the end button I can't shake the weird ache in my bones and I have to wonder, is this guy somehow connected to Mikael?

Leonidas will be here to pick me up any minute now and I can't find my other fucking shoe! How does a grown woman with no pets or children lose her damn shoes? It isn't like I kick them in different directions when... I sit back on my heels. I put both shoes in one spot. I know I did.

A quick spell recitation and I know there hasn't been anyone in my room or the house. Another spell to make the shoe shine a light to reveal itself and a spot inside my wall starts to shine in the shape of my shoe. How the fuck? "Ok, I don't know if this is a house spirit of some sort or rats or what. I am willing to work with you, but not tonight and taking my things is not the way to deal with me. I'll wear a different pair tonight and make that one stop shining," I wave my hand to null the spell, "but you need to put it back where you found it. If you don't want to speak in person, you are welcome to use a sheet of paper and leave a note. I would prefer friendliness." After talking to possibly just weird rats I get up and walk to the closet to get a different pair of heels only to find that they are all out of sorts and there isn't two matching shoes anywhere near each other. Which is why when Leonidas comes in he find me on hands and knees in the closet mumbling about assholes fucking up my shoes.

My heart nearly exits my body when he says, "As nice as the view is from here, is there a reason you are on the floor in the closet mumbling to yourself?"

"Holy hell Leonidas! Make some noise when you walk!"

He laughs as he walks over to crouch down beside me, "I did. You didn't hear me because you were busy grumbling. So, why are you down here grumbling?"

"Because Something took one of my shoes into the wall over there and left the rest of them all mixed up and finding a matching pair is a pain. Do you have any idea how much it would suck wearing shoes by two different makers? Even if they were essentially the same the differences between makers would make it agonizing."

"Something took one of your shoes into the wall? Did I hear that right?"

"Yes. I had a pair out that I had worn recently and planned to wear tonight. But the mate to it is in the wall which I figured out with magic after I realized that I hadn't left them scattered."

"Hmm, we'll revisit that. For now, what shoe are you trying to find a mate for?"

"This one." I hold up a black platform shoe with four inch heels, "The brand name is Kani."

I watch in amazement as he quickly sorts through the shoes and finds the mate to my shoe. He stands and offers a hand to help me up which I accept and then he keeps his arm out for me to lean on as I slip on my shoes. He smiles at me, "Ready to go?"

"Yes, thank you." We start out of my room as I tell him, "You do make a very good knight. Thank you for finding my shoe."

"I am always here for you. Whether it is finding mis-sorted shoes or slaying beasts, I am your guy."

My heart melts as he says that because he just keeps proving it. I mean, he rebuilt our entire house for us and charged as little as possible, even doing a lot of the work himself. He is always there when I need him. We step out of the house and I wave a hand to lock the house up as we walk to his truck. He opens the door and waits as I get myself in before gently shutting the door.

After he gets us going I ask him, "So, where are we going anyway?"

"We are going to see the Trans-Siberian Orchestra."

"Really? I love them! I've never been to see them. I thought they only played around Christmas though?"

"You are correct. They do. November through December."

"It's that late in the year already? It seems like it was just summer..."

"It is. You have been pretty busy this year."

He parks the truck and I wait as he comes around to my door because I know it gives him pleasure to pamper me and I like the feeling of being pampered. Walking into the venue I start to notice all the decorations for the holidays up everywhere. How have I been missing this? I suppose I have been preoccupied a lot lately. Which reminds me, I have a whole talk to have with Leonidas. We get through the crowd and make it to our seats. Looking around I put a sound shield around the two of us.

"I have some things I need to tell you. I know this isn't the ideal place but I haven't actually seen you in a minute. The stuff is kind of important. So, do you want to know now or would you prefer to wait till later?"

He leans back in his chair, "Tell me now so I can enjoy my time with you and not have to worry about some talk later."

I go over everything with him, giving him the shortest possible version while still including the pertinent details. Like the fact that his mom was a guardian. He stops me at the explosion though, "Wait. Someone that was supposed to be backup for you, that was backup for my mom tried to injure whoever sat in that chair next out of spite because you wouldn't let her bully you?"

"Essentially, yes."

"You aren't going to trust her or work with her, right?"

"Trust her, no. But I need to find out more about this gig before I flat out refuse to work with her. I think I am going to talk to Father Neally some more and possibly Nia. She was the one that pointed it out to me. She also took my side."

"How do you know it wasn't her that set the trap?"

"Her magic has a different feel to it. We all kind of have a certain feel to our magic, a flavor if you will. Her magic and Lacey's magic taste different. Something like the difference, in this case, between unseasoned meatloaf and curry. There really is no mistaking one for the other."

"I see. It is better to be armed with as much knowledge as possible before making a decision. As for my mother, she obviously has always had a lot of secrets. I can't even really say that I blame her. Keeping herself to herself probably kept her safe more than once."

"I think it did. So you are okay with all this?"

"I don't know if okay is the right word, because I very much dislike you being in danger. But. I feel like you can handle whatever comes your way and I am here for you any time you need me."

I lay my head on his shoulder, "You are entirely too good for the likes of me. What are you going to do when I fall for you?"

I feel his arms wrap around me as he says, "Catch you and never let you go."

The lights dim and the first few notes start to play, I think I could stay here forever.

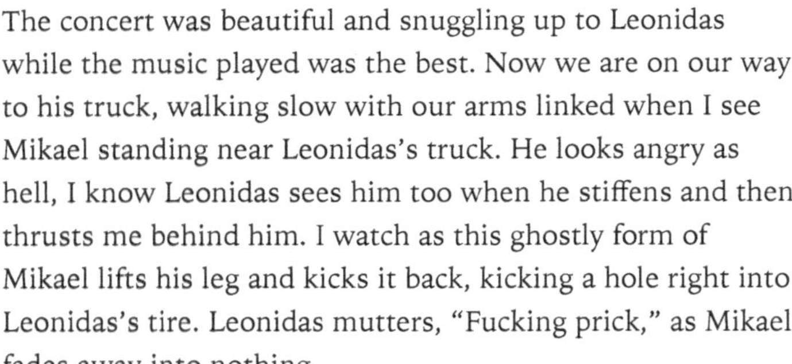

The concert was beautiful and snuggling up to Leonidas while the music played was the best. Now we are on our way to his truck, walking slow with our arms linked when I see Mikael standing near Leonidas's truck. He looks angry as hell, I know Leonidas sees him too when he stiffens and then thrusts me behind him. I watch as this ghostly form of Mikael lifts his leg and kicks it back, kicking a hole right into Leonidas's tire. Leonidas mutters, "Fucking prick," as Mikael fades away into nothing.

Ten minutes later the tire is changed and we are on our way back home when Leonidas asks, "Does he do that a lot?"

"As often as he can I think. But I feel like once is to often with how much I don't want to see him."

"Does he always try to destroy things?"

"Um, no. Usually he talks shit or looks sad before disappearing. I think seeing you with me bothers him. It bothers him a lot."

"Good. We need to find a way to stop him being such a problem."

"I am beginning to agree. I still don't want to kill him, but I am open to other suggestions."

"Tie my hands and then tell me you're open to suggestions. Ugh."

Fourteen

Scarlett

I sent the messages out this morning, both of them replied saying they would be here this afternoon, once she leaves to meet with the guy to talk about books. I think the guy is interested in her, not talking books but she wasn't hearing me. I'm not really concerned because what's he going to do that she couldn't handle? Nothing. Besides, it's a public meeting, it will be fine.

What will not be fine is if one of us acts a fool. Leonidas's mother died that night so I don't know if he remembers any of what she said from what she was seeing. But I remember what Jasmine told me and…I hear knocking at the door.

Opening the door I find Leonidas and Sebastian, glaring at each other. "Get in here! And stop glaring at each other." I listen for their footsteps and the door shutting as I lead the way to the living area. We all are going to have to work together if she is going to succeed. I seat myself in a chair facing a love seat and a couch so I can see both at the same time. We haven't replaced the chair that got blown up yet so there is just a scorch mark on the floor there.

When they are finally seated I say, "Now, I'm going to need you both to set your testosterone aside for… a while. Do you understand?"

Leonidas tugs his collar as he nods. Sebastian looks smug though and I feel like I am going to need to wipe the smirk off his face. "Recently your mother, Leonidas, told Jasmine some things. I don't know how much you remember of that as it was not a great night for you, I'm sorry for your loss." He nods as I go on, "The one thing she said that has been circling my brain since was the bit about keeping her heart open so she does not turn into what is after her. Or something to that effect. The important part is that her heart needs to remain open. How much do either of you know about her past?"

Leonidas says, "I know that her husband was a piece of work. I smelled her blood in various places in the place she lived before she ever came home. It was part of why I hung around instead of cleaning up and leaving. I needed to see her. Had she not run into Mikael that night I would have turned her myself just to have the opportunity to continue being around her. Her husband tried to buy his life by selling us hers. She was somewhere else entirely and he tried to bargain with her life for his. I let my guys play with him. And I know her aunt was no better."

"And you Sebastian?"

"I confess, I know precious little about her. I haven't had as much opportunity to spend time with her as I would like. There appears to be a lot that I don't know."

I nod, "Well, Leonidas has given you the short version of this life. Her past lives were not great either. She is pretty certain that Mikael murdered her in her first one—"

Leonidas explodes, "Then why the fuck won't she let any of us kill him?"

Sebastian chuckles, "Maybe we could get along all right."

"Well, it seems we all agree on one thing at least. Her only answer has been that she doesn't want to kill the one person that has known her since the first time she came to this planet. I would like to say I understand but I really don't. It is her quirk and if one of us kills him it needs to appear that we did it by accident, possibly in the heat of a moment. I know he older and stronger than both of you, but that is not the case with me. I am both older and stronger than he and he knows it." I shake my head, "That is not the point here. The point is that we seem to be caught up in something much bigger than any of us and I am pretty sure that Jasmine is the team the world needs to win. We," I make a circle with my finger in the air to include all of us, "very probably have a direct effect on the outcome based on our actions in our relationships with her. If I understand correctly, she needs to love and be loved even if she isn't entirely sure what to do with that."

Leonidas nods, "That is what I got from what mom said."

"Yes. So, the point here is that if she gets her heart broken again it could be bad for the world. I don't mind being just one of her lovers. Which is a little odd as I am jealous as fuck by nature, but that isn't the point. The point is, I love her. I am here for the long haul. My question for you, and the reason I asked you here today, is what do you intend? We are early enough into things that I think she would probably get over losing one or even two of us right now. It needs to be now or not for a long time though. I realize this is asking a lot in a new relationship. Especially one as far outside the usual as this. But you both need to make your choices and act accordingly before she gets so attached that she can't go back."

Leonidas smiles, "I made my choice the night I saw her kill one of my men. I had sent him to bring her to me. She led him into a secluded area, he had no clue that he was walking into her trap. She killed him quickly and with no remorse, it was the sexiest thing I had ever seen and I was hooked right then. There is no turning back or away for me. I need her as much as she needs us."

"And you Sebastian?"

"I would prefer to have more time before admitting to it, but I am all in for her. From the moment I saw her walking out of Mikael's bedroom mad as hell that he wouldn't have sex with her, she was all I could think about. I could no more walk away from her than either of you could."

I nod, "Good. Ok. That being all settled, you know that if the two of you continue to have beef she is going to feel bad and obligated to choose. I will stuff the two of you into a box and seal it until you learn to get along before I let you continue to act the fool knowing it will hurt her and cause her to doubt herself."

Sebastian cocks his head to one side, "What would you tell her is the reason we both disappeared?"

Grinning I tell him, "That you two went on a trip to bond."

I watch their eyes widen and I laugh as it sinks in for them that I could absolutely get away with that. Sebastian faces Leonidas, "Care to go have a drink?"

"I think I would like that." Leonidas cuts his eyes at me, "And it might be safer anyway. Thanks for the talk Scarlett, you have my number if you need anything."

Sebastian stands when Leonidas does and says, "Yes. Good talk. You know my number. Prefer not to be shoved in a box. Have a great evening."

I try to laugh less as they leave. They sure do get silly about things when they are reminded that someone can and will take them to task.

Jasmine

I arrive at the café that Hake requested we meet at. I have some blooded wine in a flask in my purse, so I plan to buy a cold coffee and swap things in the bathroom. As long as I buy one of their plastic cups that aren't transparent all will work out just fine. Walking in I don't see him just yet and that works out just fine for me. I order a drink at the counter and wait for it. Once I have it I make a beeline for the bathroom. Luckily no one else is in there as I dump the coffee drink in the toilet and pour my wine in the empty cup. Slapping the lids back in place I shove my empty container back into my purse and flush the toilet before exiting the stall. A glance in the mirror and I exit the bathroom. I see Hake in line as he notices me with a drink already in my hand. He frowns at my drink which is odd. Why would he frown at that? Oh, maybe because I was in the bathroom with it? I'm sure that does seem odd, but he is human and I can't exactly just tell him why. Although, I know human women take their drinks to because men are not trustworthy anywhere near as often as they should be.

With a shrug I go sit at a table near the window so I can watch people walk by. Hake makes it to the table with his drink, "Hello! I am so glad you came Jasmine! I would have gotten your drink for you though, there was no need to buy it yourself."

I frown, "That's ok, I got it. So, do you have any good book recommendations for me? Any home reno books you think I should try?"

Hake taps his cup like he is annoyed, "I do, but I would like to know more about you. What you do. What makes you tick. I want to know Jasmine."

"Um, what? Why are you being weird Hake? I thought we were getting together to talk books. Not me. That's weird. Do you have a different idea about this? Did we miscommunicate?"

He smiles but it doesn't reach his eyes, "No, no, of course not. I just want to get to know you so I can give you better book recommendations."

My intuition is pinging off the charts and I feel a shadow of an itch in my bones. It's time for me to beat a hasty retreat. I grab my bag and stand, "I think I am going to go. This was weird, let's not do it again."

I am turning to leave when Hake grabs my arm. "I want you to stay."

I look down at his hand on my arm, "That is just too damn bad. Get your hand off me now before I rip it off and feed it to you."

His eyes narrow, "You are making a big mistake. Sit back down and talk to me. I didn't say you could leave yet."

He tries to yank me back to sitting and then I notice the power he is building. The son of a dickface is a damned witch! Oh fuck him twice! I slam a shield around him that will keep anything he is thinking about unleashing at me from hitting me or anyone else in here as I snatch my arm out of his hand, "You don't own me and I will ruin your whole damn day if you come anywhere near me ever again. Fuck all the way off Hake."

As I walk out the door I hear various people cheering and clapping. Shit. I did not mean to attract that much attention. It's fine. I won't come back to this place any time soon. I see Hake running out to catch up to me as I get in my car. I shield it and start the engine. He hits the trunk as I drive away. Fucking jackass. I thought I was going to have a book friend. I should have known. I should have known that if a man is paying me any attention it is completely because he wants in my pants.

Uggghhhh. I want rip his whole damn throat out, save some other poor woman the trouble. But that is so much more trouble than I want to deal with. Not to mention all the paperwork. Time in prison. He just isn't worth it.

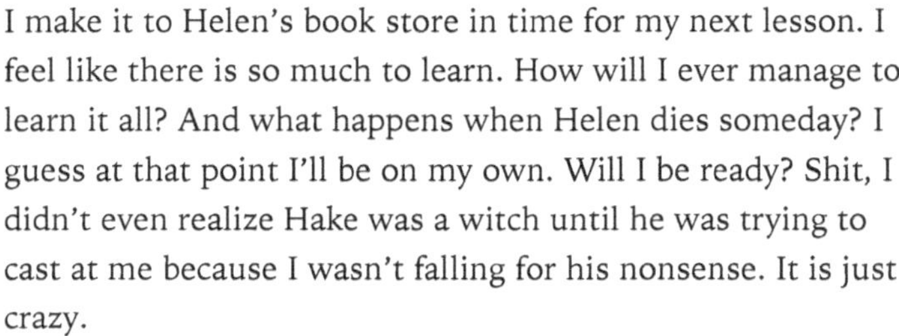

I make it to Helen's book store in time for my next lesson. I feel like there is so much to learn. How will I ever manage to learn it all? And what happens when Helen dies someday? I guess at that point I'll be on my own. Will I be ready? Shit, I didn't even realize Hake was a witch until he was trying to cast at me because I wasn't falling for his nonsense. It is just crazy.

I feel a buzzing on my skin and just a few seconds later I see Mikael's shade watching me. I flip him off just because. I know he sees it because the bastard smiles at me. Inside the book store I take a deep breath and try to call myself as I walk down the hall to the classroom. I see Helen working at setting up some things for our lessons today and I am just so grateful that Leonidas brought me here and she was working that night. She looks up and smiles as I walk in the room, "Jasmine! Hello! How was your week? Did you get any practice in?"

"I did. Practice that is. And, I got some surprise practice just a little while ago. Plus, Mikael is still sending his shades to bother me."

Her brows raise as she says, "Surprise practice?"

I explain what happened with Hake and she clucks, "Bad form, hiding what you are from someone you are interested in. But then, judging by the rest of his behavior he isn't the terribly interested in being a decent witch or person."

"No, I don't think he is."

"Now, this shade Mikael keeps sending at you. I am guessing you don't know who he has sending this at you?"

"No. I don't even know where Mikael is. Honestly, until the break in most people didn't believe he was still alive."

"Hmm, yes. Most will be very limited by what they can see and have evidence of, even in the magical community. With all the scientific advancements we have and people that are part of a community that most of humanity knows nothing about, still they won't believe someone lived through an event just because they can't find them." She shakes her head, "Well, for now let's get on with some learning. You need to expand your knowledge of general magic so you will have the building blocks to create the bigger things."

Two hours later I have done small magics till I feel like my fingers could bleed over it when Helen says, "That's enough for tonight. You are doing so well Jasmine! I think I will walk out with you tonight. If that Mikael is waiting for you I'll send him back with a bug in his ear."

"How do you do that?"

"Hmm, well, the short of it is that I return him to his sender with a tag and a stinger. The stinger will distract the sender as the tag slips in and attaches, giving me a way to recognize them."

"How will the tag show up? Is there a way for them to find it and get rid of it before you can see it?"

"Not really. If you don't see a tag when it is attaching, they are damn near impossible for anyone but the sender of the tag to find. However, the tags I am capable of doing only allow me to recognize them if they are in my vicinity. I couldn't follow them back to their location."

"What is the difference? Would I be able to track someone that way?"

"Oh yes, I think you would. The difference is mostly intent and power behind the tracker. That is the power I can put behind it, but you could put so much more. You watch as I do this, I know you will be able to pick it up. The spell is easy."

I hold the door open for her as we leave the building. We aren't halfway to my car when Mikael appears a few feet ahead of us. I do my best to keep an eye on him while focusing on what Helen's magic does. He is mostly talking smack about my hanging out with an old lady. I follow her magic as it leaves her hands and hits him in the chest. His face is comical. Then he seems to be snatched by a rubber band back to wherever he originated. I think Helen is right, I could absolutely do that and it would be hilarious. "Helen, I think you are the most amazing and generous witch I have ever met. I can do that, I know I could."

Helen blushes and waves away my compliment, "Oh stop. Anyone else could teach you the same or better. You are a marvelous student and I am so lucky that I will get to say I had any sort of influence on you. You will be a credit to myself and your future teachers."

"Future teachers? Bah, what would I need with more teachers after you?"

Her lips take on a wry twist, "Well, for starters all the offensive style magic that Hekate has been teaching you?"

I duck my head, "Oh. So you know about that?"

"Of course I do. She and I talked it over. We both know that I am great as a starting point and I can give you a working knowledge of the basics that will serve you well in the future as you start to create your own spells."

"I am sure that is a long way off. I feel like I still have so much to learn. So much that I haven't even begun to understand yet."

She shakes her head no at me, "You are so much farther than you realize. One day, as you look back on things, you will realize just how amazing it is that you have done all you have done in such a short time. For now, just be easier on yourself. You went through a lot of hard things. I am getting entirely too sappy. He won't be back tonight. That sting will have him hurting for a while. You go ahead and go home. I'll see you soon. You and I have that lunch coming up, and I can't wait to show you the place."

I thank her and head to my car though I listen to make sure she gets back in the book store. She wouldn't like it if I were too obvious with watching to make sure that she made it in safe and I can respect that. Now, back to my sanctuary.

Fifteen

Jasmine

I am restless today and I need to go out somewhere. I should probably wait till tonight and hunt but I have blood in the fridge. I am not going hungry. After pacing through the house yet again I decide to go visit Helen's book store. I don't have lessons right now but if I remember correctly, they were getting a shipment in this morning. My course decided I grab my purse and fish out my keys on the way out the door.

I feel better just for going out the door and I know that an outing is exactly what I need to get me back on track. I have spent entirely too much time trying to figure out how to use that damn key to get into the library. I wonder if it is possible that the explosion set off a security thing and I don't know how to reset it? Or, what if the chair wasn't the only thing that Lacey messed with that day?

Maybe I should go talk to Father Neally soon. Maybe he has an idea of why I can't find it. Not today though. Today is a day for a relaxing visit to my favorite book store. Old me is still in awe of the fact that I have not only a favorite bookstore but friends. I am not getting my ass kicked on the regular because I breathed wrong. For all this fuckery, my life is still worlds better than it ever was prior.

A sigh of contentment escapes as I pull into a parking space at the store. Going in I head straight for the counter, I had some books on order and I can't wait to read them. I am still going to look at the new books, but I want to check on these and talk to the witch in charge anyway. They are so nice. I know they must get tired of my face. Alice smiles as I walk over and then reaches under the counter to pull out a stack of books with a smile she slides them across to me. "Here you go. We knew you would be by today, even if you thought you would wait."

I laugh and squeal with delight as I check over the books. Sarra Cannon's last book in her series is in the stack, I can't wait to see how it ends! One of Michelle Pillow's Warlock MacGregor books is sitting over K.F. Breene's A Ruin of Roses, and Anne Bishop's latest book from the world of The Others!

"I can't wait to start reading! But, I have to check the new shipment first. Did you all get them out already?"

Alice looks around and whispers, "Yes. We were dead this morning and so we just used magic to put them out. So much faster."

"Yes! Ok. I am going to go look, hold my babies till I come back?"

"Of course. Enjoy!"

Wandering the stacks and I find three more books before I can convince myself to stop. I love being able to buy books and know that they won't be destroyed as soon as I take them in the house. I thought once I was free of him that I would be free of the worry and the memories, but that isn't how it's working. I still wake up at night when I hear a noise and I am terrified it is him coming home, that all this has been a dream. I can only hope that it fades with the passage of time. Or that I find a great vampire therapist eventually… Maybe I should read some self help books too?

I'll save that for another day. For now, I am buying all these books and I am going home to tuck myself into bed and devour them. Alice rings me up with a smile and I soon have my purchases in a bag as I leave the book store with a wave and run directly into someone. I turn to apologize and help them up but to my surprise it's Hake. Stepping to the side I let him help himself up as I ask, "What are you doing here Hake?"

"I wanted to explain. I know what you are," he looks around to make sure we aren't overheard, "I know. It's ok. I'm a witch. But I feel drawn to you. Like fate is pushing me to be with you. I just can't stay away from you."

He goes on telling me how he thinks we are meant to be and all I can hear are the alarms in my head clanging for all they are worth. I slap a shield over myself, I'm not worried about the bookstore, they have plenty of shielding to take care of anything this guy could put out. I should have thrown up shields as soon as I saw it was him.

"Hake, no. I don't feel called or drawn or pulled or any other thing to you. Except repelled. Definitely feeling repelled by you. How did you even find me here?"

He looks surprised at my question, like he didn't even hear the rest, "Oh, I followed you the other day. I thought I would give you some time to cool down. Plus, I had to go to a meeting and you were already gone by the time I got back. Sneaky girl!" He grins at me like what he said was any kind of cute.

"You followed me? Hake, that is not ok. I told you I don't want anything to do with you and I meant it. Get away from me."

He steps closer, "Oh Jasmine,—"

I put a hand up to stop him coming closer, "No! You come any closer to me and I throw you across the parking lot. You fuck right off with all your bullshit. You don't get to have me because you feel pulled to me or whatever stupid-ass word you use for your delusions. The fucking audacity! If you come anywhere near me again I will not hesitate to end you. This is your only fucking warning." I turn to leave and I hear him run at me. I wait till he is nearly on me before swinging my fist a full arc to hit him in the face. The look of surprise on his face makes all this nearly worth it. Then he crumples to the ground. He is mostly on the sidewalk but I feel like I should at least let Alice know. I open the door and catch her attention, gesturing that I need her out here. She nods and locks the register before coming around the counter and heading my way.

She looks at me in confusion when she sees Hake laying on the ground. I give her the quick explanation of what happened and she nods, telling me, "You go on home. I'll glamour him to look like a large rock and we'll leave him there. If he isn't gone in a couple hours when I get done with my shift, I'll call the cops and tell them that there is a strange man unconscious in front of the store. Be safe, witch weirdos are some of the worst. It sucks, but it is always extra awful when we go offsides."

She waves a hand at him and he appears to be a rock. I thank her and hurry across the parking lot to my car. I decide right then to glamour it to look different to Hake every time he sees it. Different body style, tag, and color. I don't want him accidentally finding me by spotting my car. Getting in, I start the car and point myself toward home. I want to be far away from here when that asshat wakes up.

Mikael

I watch Jasmine leave the parking lot like her tail is on fire. She obviously recognized Hake and what's more, she made it very clear she already told him she doesn't want him. How very interesting. Hake must have met her elsewhere prior to today and fallen in love with her.

Trying to take what is mine, knowing that I will find out eventually. He had to know. Rage spreads through my body. I watched the witch cover him with the illusion of a rock. Now the question becomes, do I want him to know I know about his duplicity?

Vigo clears his throat, "Sir, do you want me to collect him for you?"

"No. I want him to lay there and wake up in pain. We will go home now. I am content that Jasmine saw through him.

Though my rage is unparalleled with Hake. I want his punishment to fit his crime."

Vigo looks up at me, hunger in his eyes, "Would you, would you care to take some of that rage out on me sir?"

I reach over to run a hand down his face and then grip his chin hard, drawing his face close to mine, I whisper, "As forward as you are, I think you definitely need a punishment." I feel his hands drifting up my chest and I give him a shake, "Did I say you could touch me? It's the paddle for you when we get home. Maybe I'll let you take the cage off before."

Vigo draws in a breath and his eyes nearly glow with excitement as he says, "Yes sir, I'm sorry sir. I deserve your punishment." A smile plays at his lips as he says, "We should get home now. Wouldn't want me thinking I was going to get away with my transgressions, would we?"

I release his chin with a shove as I smile, "No. We wouldn't. Get in the car Vigo. You can suck me on the way home."

He runs to the car, opens my door and then runs around to get in the passenger side. I may have to drive slowly all the way home.

Jasmine

When I get home I see Scarlett and Chloe are already here and I am just so glad I will have someone to vent to about all this shit. Getting out I walk into the house and I can hear them talking in the living area, their voices soothe me and I call out, "Honeys, I'm home! And I have shitty stories to share!"

Chloe calls out, "I've brought the good wine!"

Scarlett says, "I've got a glass waiting to be filled just for you! Come sit!"

I set my books on the table near the door along with my purse and I give the door a gentle kick to close it. A magic zap locks it as I head for the living area and the wine.

Scarlett pats the spot next to her as I walk in and Chloe grins at the two of us as I sit and Scarlett hugs me close. I return the hug, it feels really good to be hugged by someone that cares about me. I hold on longer than I should and she just lets me, keeps her arms wrapped around me till I let go. When I do release her she picks up the glass she said was waiting for me and holds it out to Chloe who fills it perfectly. Scarlett passes it to me and I take a sip as they watch me expectantly. "This is sweet. And blooded. It's not a red. Is this," I take another sip, "is this a moscato?"

Chloe laughs and says, "Yes! Isn't is great? I found a vampire that makes his own wines and then bloods them himself. He said it is time consuming but his clientele is small. He is thinking about taking on young vampires, employing them to blood the wine. I think that is great, because I want him to keep making this. I love sweet wines but they are so finicky when it comes to mixing with blood."

"Um, I think we need an introduction. This is fantastic. I want to get more to keep here at the house."

Scarlett nods, "Yes. I told her the same. She already promised she would. And Eason is going to introduce him to some new vampires. He should have plenty of good help to keep up the supply."

Chloe asks, "So, what happened to you while you were out?"

"Oh, you know, I had nearly forgot about it after the hug and the awesome wine. So," I turn to look at Scarlett, "you remember I went to meet Hake at the café to talk books and he wanted to talk sweet at me instead because of course he did?" She nods and I turn so I can see Chloe too, "Well, guess who ambushed me outside Helen's book store tonight? I came walking out and ran right into him, knocked him on his ass and then he starts spouting all this nonsense about drawn to me and fate and uuugggh! What is wrong with him? What's wrong with me that I attract so many whack jobs and I can't even spot them at a distance?"

"Oh honey," Scarlett's arm slips around my shoulders and she pulls me in for a quick hug, when she releases me she keeps her hand on my back rubbing small circles.

"It was nice knocking him out and leaving him laying there. Don't worry, I told Alice in the store. She glamoured him to look like a rock so no passersby would be concerned. But damn, it's not like I have a gold plated pussy or something! He never even had the chance to get close to my pussy. What is up with these assholes?"

Chloe starts giggling. I look over at her with my eyes narrowed and Scarlett makes a choking noise. Glaring at the two of them I ask, "What is so damn funny?"

Chloe laughs out loud as Scarlett squeals, "Gold plated pussy," and also starts laughing. I can't even be mad about that and their laughter is infectious, I start laughing with them.

We manage to calm down eventually and Chloe says, "As hilarious as the way you phrased that was, how did he find you at that book store?"

"I asked the same question. That jackass literally said he followed me from our meetup. The only reason he didn't follow me home that day was because he had a meeting to go to that stopped him from being there when I left. I glamoured my car to looked different to him. Hopefully that will make it more difficult for him to find me. And maybe he will have a concussion and forget all about me?" They both raise their brows at me. "Yeah. I know. But it's a nice thought."

"We'll just need to be more aware. He's only human. He can't do much," Scarlett says and I flinch. Of course she notices that and lasers in on it, "What? What was that? He isn't human is he? Oh for fuck's sake. What is he?"

With a grimace I say, "Witch."

She groans, "Well, looks like you get to go about reinforcing the shields on this place. And, you need to stay shielded yourself when you go out."

"I know. I know. And I will. He was hiding it from me before is the only reason I didn't know until he got mad that I wasn't having our meetup be a date."

Sixteen

Jasmine

I answer the door to find Chloe, she gives me an exuberant hug, saying "We are going out to play hunt a rapist, want to join us? It's so much fun and there is always so much to eat. We could really use the extra mouth. You would be doing us a favor if you came."

"Ha," I shake my head, "I'm sure. But no. I want to stay home and read. I have a lot of thinking to do."

"I understand. But you should come out and have fun too."

"I will. I just want it to be a little less of a gamble before I start wandering around deleting shitholes. Make sure I don't have anyone following me looking to put an end to my shenanigans."

She purses her lips and nods, "I see your point."

"Come on, you can sit with me while Scarlett finishes getting ready. Want a drink?"

Just as we sit down Scarlett walks in, "Hello! Jasmine, are you sure you won't go?"

"I'm sure. But, I do want to talk to you and the guys in the morning, if that is a good time for you?"

"Sure, what's it about?"

"Oh, just the same stuff I told you about from when I saw Leonidas's mom last. I've been mulling things over and I want to keep everyone in the loop so to speak."

"Ah, I see. Come on Chloe, let's get out of here. See you in the morning Jasmine." She blows a kiss at me on the way out. Yeah, I think I could fall for her really hard if I just let myself. But that's why I need to talk to everyone before I go changing rules they might not want to change. They leave and I settle in on the couch with my drink and my books for a long night of bliss since I messaged the guys earlier.

It is near morning when everyone finds their way to the house. I see Leonidas pause after getting out of his truck, staring up at the house for long moments before he starts for the front door. I feel bad for living here, knowing it was his mother's home for so long but I can't live elsewhere. This place is home. Plus there is the matter of the library... which I still can't find. It makes me wonder. I don't think it should be this difficult to find. I'll call Father Neally later this morning, see if he might know something.

I walk over and open the door before Leonidas can knock, his surprise at the door opening is quickly replaced with a happy smile as he says, "Hello sexy, how's your morning going?"

I wrap my arms around him and draw him in the house as I say, "It is just getting better and better. How was work?"

"It was good. This house is finished except for the interior. But we will move on to the next one until this one sells. Once we have the requests for finishes and what not, we'll swoop in and finish it up."

"Sounds great, come sit with me while we wait for the others to get here."

He sits in a chair but when I attempted to move to a couch to sit nearby he grabs my waist and lifts me into the air, depositing me on his lap. "I haven't seen you in entirely too long and no one else is here yet. I got here early just for this and I plan to take advantage of the time alone."

"I like the way you think sir," I tell him as I sort myself to sitting facing him with a knee on each side of his hips. "It has been entirely too long since we had a hot make out session while we waited."

He grins and slips his hands down to grip my hips as he leans forward to kiss me. The moment our lips touch it's like wildfire through my body. The passing of time goes unnoticed until we hear a knock at the door and come up for air. I yell toward the door, "Be right there!" I scramble to get up and Leonidas is zero help. Then I realize all of my clothing is out of place. Shooting him a look I button my shorts, shoving bra and shirt back into place. His grin is unrepentant as he readjusts himself.

I make it to the door, opening it to find Sebastian, he smiles, opening his arms and saying, "Hey babe. How's things?" I jump into his arms and he hugs me tight whispering, "Have I told you how hot you look with your lips swollen from kisses and your hair mussed? Sexy enough to eat."

My core quivers at his words, as it is already on fire from Leonidas's kisses. "You haven't, but I sure love hearing you say it. Now, set me down, you are the second to arrive and Scarlett should be here any moment now."

He nips my neck causing me to shiver as he sets me back on the ground. I hold onto his arms for a moment just to catch my balance and then pull him inside, giving him a push toward the living area when I see Chloe pulling up to drop off Scarlett. Chloe waves from the car before she drives off and I watch Scarlett walk up to the house. Her curves give me palpitations. The roundness of her hips and thighs, the softness of her arms, the pillows of her breasts; all of it covering the solid muscle of a woman that can kill with ease or fuck the hell right out of you.

"I see I am the last to arrive."

"You are, but you know what they say, save the best for last, right?"

She slips a hand round the back of my neck and the other around my waist, pulling me into a sweet, slow kiss that sets me on fire in all the right ways. I run my hands over her curves and press myself against her. We break for air and she kisses her way down my throat as the hand on my waist slips down to cup my ass. She nips my neck and draws back, "We should probably go inside, you said I was the last one here."

I only understand that her lips are not on my neck anymore and force my eyes open, "Hmm?"

She chuckles, "We need to go in. The guys are probably going nuts smelling what I do to you."

"Oh! Oh yes. We should." I stand up on my own, bringing my hands back to myself as she releases me, "Phew. You are a hella distraction." Rolling my shoulders I lead the way to the living area where both men are waiting with matching smirks though their eyes speak of hunger. I sit in the only other chair because I don't want to sit next to one and have the others thinking I have chosen sides or something. Scarlett seats herself and I look at the three of them, I don't know what good I did in another life to deserve this but wow, I am a lucky woman. "Ok, so, I wanted to talk to all of you because after talking to Hekate and Helen about what your mother said Leonidas, it looks like everything I had asked of you all has to change." I look out the window, this is so much harder than I thought it would be. "Um, so, they say I have to keep my heart open. I know that everything I have asked of you all is to keep my heart safe. Closed off from everyone, but safe. Since that doesn't seem to be an option and I don't want to become that which seeks to own me, I think it is only fair that I offer you all a get out free card. If this isn't for you, if you don't want to stay in this relationship with everyone here, then I understand. I can't even blame you." I look back at them to see all of them watching me, looking so serious, "My life is a lot and I— if you were to stay— this would all change. It would bring feelings into it, so much more than I have allowed myself to have up to now. So, um, if you want to, to walk away," I take a breath, I didn't expect that last part to be so hard to say, "I could survive it right now and either way I wouldn't hold it against you. The thing is, I am kind of... damaged. If you decide to stay and change your mind later, I'll let you walk away because I would not want to keep you against your will. I just ask that you let me down as easy as possible and well, do it now rather than later if at all possible."

Leonidas stands and walks across the room to kneel in front of me, "I told you that I am here. For as long as you will have me. I knew I wanted to be with you the night my clan murdered your husband and set you free. I have been yours ever since that first night. I am yours, however you will have me." He lays his head in my lap and wraps his arms around my waist.

Sebastian sighs, "Well, way to make the rest of us look cheap there Leo. Jasmine, I wanted you the moment I saw you walking frustrated and angry out of Mikael's bedroom. I haven't been able to get you out of my mind since then and once I got a taste of you my fate was sealed. You could banish me from your side but I would perish from the lack of the sunlight that is you. Do with me as you will."

Tears are flowing down my face as Scarlett says, "Jasmine, I'm yours. I won't give you pretty speeches to make you cry. But I am here for the long run. You don't have to worry that I am going to ditch you for the next fun thing. I don't even mind the danger so long as I have you."

I cover my face with my hands, "I don't deserve any of you."

Leonidas lifts his head and moves his hands to my shoulders, "I think we can all agree, we don't deserve you. Now, let's have some drinks and celebrate this strange new land of our relationships with you. Because honestly, each of us feels like they have won a whole jackpot."

"Ok, but can someone bring me a towel to clean up all these tears? Being a vampire has some serious drawbacks…"

Leonidas laughs, "That means you are on drink duty 'Bastian. I know where the towels are."

I hear the two of them walk out and Scarlett says in a quiet voice, "We really are the lucky ones. And now we have a chance at you loving us. You have no idea what a gift you are giving each of us."

Without uncovering my face, "Yeah, wait until you hear about the library job and the fact that I can't find the library entrance…"

Mikael

Hake has just arrived and Vigo is escorting him in. I am curious as to what excuses he plans to provide. He has no idea that I saw him trying to claim Jasmine as his own and I think I will keep it that way.

Vigo is noisy as he nears my study, his way of making sure I know that he is near with our guest. The door swings silently inwards and Vigo steps aside to allow Hake entrance. I can smell Hake's nerves as he walks in. My girl has a hella punch, his bruises are vibrant.

Vigo asks, "Sir, shall I get you drinks?"

"Yes. Make Hake's a double, he's stressed."

I watch Hake while I wait for Vigo to return with our drinks. He could have made them here but it's more fun for him to make them elsewhere while I watch Hake sweat. I am surprised he is still mindful that I don't want to talk business until I have my drink in hand. His sweat reeks of fear and I find it exciting. Perhaps when he is gone I'll have Vigo sit there while I fuck his face so I can smell the fear sweat Hake is leaving all over the chair.

Vigo returns with our drinks, passing them out quickly and asking if there is anything else I will need. "We will be working more once Hake leaves. Stay near."

His eyes glitter and a small smile plays on his lips as he nods before leaving the room. I can smell the excitement in his wake. As Vigo closes the door I ask Hake, "So what news do you have for me?"

He swallows audibly before speaking, "I met her. I decided meeting her would help me to get a better read on her, to figure out what would best drive her to you. I even arranged to have an argument with her and cause her to be violent. She is easily angered, isn't she?" I nod my agreement and he continues, "She is the one that did this to my face. I have learned that she goes to a particular bookstore weekly, sometimes multiple times weekly. It will be an easy thing for me to follow her and find where she resides now. And I found that she isn't getting enough training, as she didn't immediately know me for a witch."

"That is all well and good, but what does that do for me?"

"It gets me closer to bringing her to you. I will ramp up the attacks on her psyche and see if we can't get rid of some of her friends."

"She is weak where they are concerned."

"Yes, and if I get rid of some of them she will be more vulnerable to you. The ideal way would be for her to run to you for protection. That would give you power over her in a way that will be lasting. She won't know who killed her friends and she will have to stay away from them just to keep them from being killed by this thing targeting her."

Swirling the brandy in my glass I pretend to mull this over. "It sounds solid. Which friend will you start with?"

"Her book store witch friend. She interfered with a spell of mine and I would like to repay her kindness by taking her out of the equation."

"Ok. That will do for now. I expect to hear back from you by the end of the week with some better results than a bruised face."

"Yes, of course. This was just testing the waters, getting close so I could do my job better. I am ever mindful of the prize."

"See that you stay mindful. Vigo!" He must have been waiting just outside the door as he opens it almost as his name leaves my lips. "Escort Hake back to his vehicle. He has work to do."

"Yes sir. Come along Hake."

Hake shoots the rest of his brandy and says, "See you soon Mikael, with good news."

Vigo returns quickly, "Sir, do we believe any of what he had to say?"

"No. But it is better if he doesn't know that. His plan to make her friends drop like flies is a good one. I think he plans for her to run to him, but I will ensure that she seeks me out instead."

"That seems risky sir. Is she not afraid of you already?"

"Yes. But I didn't kill her friends. When she accuses me of their murder I can call Hake out and place the blame on him. He went rogue. He didn't follow orders. I'll rip out his throat in a rage and she will be grateful. Then I'll explain that he wasn't working alone and the only way to keep them safe is to stay with me. It has the bonus of getting rid of Hake too. He would never make a suitable vampire and I really don't want him to be of my line."

Vigo shivers, "I love it when you are diabolical. It makes me…hot."

"Good. His fear made me hot. Sit in that chair, I want to face fuck you while the scent of it lingers still."

Vigo races to the chair and is seated before I am standing. "Good pet."

Seventeen

Jasmine

Helen sent me an address to meet her at and I am unsure I am at the right place until I pull into the parking lot and feel a cool magic flow over me and the trash place I was seeing is gone. In its place is a lovely little restaurant and the parking is not empty as it seemed when I was driving up. This is some fancy magic here and I love it.

After finding a spot in the crowded lot I walk up and see Helen waiting for me on the sidewalk. She smiles and waves, throwing her arms around me for a hug as soon as I am close enough.

"Isn't this great?" She hooks her arm in mine, "This place caters to the entire magical community and at the same time keeps itself hidden from the humans. They have a go away spell on this place that is just amazing. Subtle yet, powerfully effective."

We make it to the entrance and I hold the door for her. She walks in ahead of me and tells the host we would like seating for two. They consult the chart and grab some things from under their stand, "Follow me please." They take us to a cozy booth with a great view. The neighborhood behind this place is wild. It is like another world entirely. I could spend hours watching but I am here to have lunch with Helen. We start with browsing the menu, and I am delighted to see a section for vampires. I scan the offerings and see boba tea. What the hell? I read the description. They have created bubbles of blood with magic and set it in a sweet wine. Fuck yes. I set my menu down, I know what I want. Helen's eyes sparkle as she sets her menu down, the server appears at our table and takes our order.

Helen says, "I thought you might be interested in the boba tea. And some of the other offerings they have available. Now that you know where this place is you will always be able to find it. This restaurant is part of a whole strip of stores and such that cater to the magical community. It is busy year round, no matter how it looks before you pull into the lot."

The server brings our food and we eat as she tells me about the area. She tells me how she grew up in the neighborhood behind this place. I love hearing her stories. I can't imagine growing up part of the magical community, but if her stories are any example, mostly it is pretty great. My boba tea is the best. I never knew so many things could be done with blood. And the little bits of magic have their own flavor.

Our lunch finished we head to the front and I insist on paying the check. Helen accepts after a minimal amount of fuss, telling me, "Fine, and thank you. I had a wonderful time. We should do this again. I'll see you Wednesday for your next lesson."

I hug her and tell her I can't wait. Handing the cashier my card and ticket I look back and wave one more time as she pushes through the doors. The cashier asks me to sign the receipt as they hand over my card. I add a nice tip and sign the bottom. I turn to leave and I see Helen stop in the middle of the parking lot like she saw something, shoving my card in my purse I start out the door. I get out the doors just in time to hear the shots and see Helen fall to the ground. Screaming, I race over to her and drop to my knees next to her, pulling her into my lap. "Tell me how to fix this. Helen, I don't know how to fix this. Can I turn you? Will that fix it? You can't leave."

I try to stop the bleeding, pressing on her shoulder, and the spot at the base of her ribs. She puts a hand on my arm, "You can't." She gasps for air or pain, I don't know which.

"Please, just hold on! I'll get help." I scream for help and people come running, "Please, you've got to help her. Please, someone fix this! She can't go, Helen, stay, please."

Someone kneels down beside me, "I'm so sorry, your friend is gone." This person holds me and lets me cry my blood tears down their shirt, Helen's blood on the both of us. Eventually some people in uniforms show up. They take Helen from me, but they let me kiss her sweet face before they take her away.

The other people in uniforms make me stay and talk to them, asking a million questions. But nobody can answer my burning question of who did this. Eventually I am released to go home. One of the officers asks me to come to their vehicle and use these wipes to clean up so the humans won't notice a woman driving around with blood on her face. They give me a couple extra wipes for on the way home.

In the car I send a group text out before I leave, telling Scarlett, Sebastian, and Leonidas that there was an incident. Because I can't type that Helen was killed. I let them know that I am going home so they don't worry too much.

When I arrive at home I get out of the car and walk inside. The house is empty and I am kind of happy it is. Moving through the house I find my bedroom and crawl into my bed, pulling the covers up to my chin. Some time later I hear a vehicle roar up. I can't be bothered to figure out who it is, seconds later Leonidas storms into my room. He takes one look at me and turns around, stomping back out the way he came. I hear the front door close and my tears falls a little faster.

I knew I was too much a burden for everyone. Better they leave now though. Then I feel someone crawling into the bed and my eyes fly open to see Leonidas, busily working at kicking his boots off before he puts his feet on the bed. He sees me watching him and says, "Oh love, I'm so sorry I wasn't here sooner."

My voice cracked and teary I tell him, "They shot her. They shot Helen. And I couldn't fix it. I asked how, she said I couldn't. Why couldn't I fix it? What good is all this magic if I can't fix things?"

His boots hit the floor at some point and next thing I know he is leaned against the headboard and he has snatched me up to lay on his chest. I listen to the rumble as he says, "There are just some things we can't fix. No matter how powerful we are. I'm so sorry love. I know Helen is important."

I hear the front door again and this time Sebastian walks in. Leonidas waves him toward me and Sebastian kicks his shoes off. Very quickly I feel him cuddled up behind me. I don't hear the door this time but Scarlett walks in and climbs onto the bed, she lays her head on my thigh and I have never in my life felt so supported. All of them dropped whatever they were doing to come here where I was grieving.

My heart is broken over Helen and so full because of these three.

Jasmine

Dressing for the funeral feels awful. I don't want to be pretty for saying a final goodbye to my dear mentor and friend. I was granted too little time with her in this life. I can only hope I will be lucky enough to know her in the next one. My lovers, they have been here mostly since the murder.

This, this has been the only time I have really missed the comfort of having a hot beverage. Tea, coffee, whatever. I miss the comfort of sitting with hands wrapped around a cup while I go through something. Prices to pay for everything I suppose. I have been staring at my closet for entirely too long. Finding something to wear is a beast. In disgust I decide on a pair of jeans paired with a black top and I have a black trench that suits my mood. Black boots and my hair braided back has me ready to go. They decided to have an evening service for her so that I could attend. I appreciate it so much that they would consider me at all. I told everyone that I want to attend this alone and they seem like they plan to respect my wishes.

I say bye to them all and leave the house. Getting in my car for the first time since she died and I drove home with her blood all over me. Someone cleaned my car for me. It makes me want to cry all over again. And reminds me to put a glamour on all of me so my tears will appear as tears. I've never had someone just do something like this for me. Is this what life is supposed to be like? I have no experience with these things. I saw things like this in books, but nobody in my life ever did things like this. Kind just because.

Heading to the funeral home I can't help but feel like this is too many funerals in such a short time. This one is being held at the funeral home, so there won't be the discomfort of being in another church. The funeral home lot is packed. Helen was well loved. Scenting the air I know I am the only vampire here. But there are witches and humans all over the place.

I make it into the building and I am unsure about viewing her. However, I don't think I could get out of this line without making a scene so I guess I will just do my best. After what seems forever it is my turn to say goodbye to her. I walk over to her casket and look down at her. She looks weird. What the hell did they do to her face? Why are her tits strapped up so fucking high? Do they do this to everyone? Fuck, I'm really glad that if I die now I'll be a cloud of bitch-dust instead of this being done to me. "Helen, I am going to find the person that murdered you and they will pay. I love you and I miss you already. I would give anything to have gone to lunch somewhere else that day."

I walk away and head for the back. I don't want to take space from people that have known her for so much longer. They should be at the front. I find my seat and listen to the service which is apparently a lot more interesting when it is ninety-five percent witches. Holy shit, they get up to things! I hear memories of Helen that make me smile and wish ever more fervently that I had gotten to know her longer. There is not a dry eye in the building by the time the stories finish, but there has been laughter in the midst of the tears and it doesn't get much better than that.

The service ends and we all file out to our cars. I have to say, this is the most orderly function I have ever been to. It is mostly women here and nobody parked like and asshole, nobody is fighting for position, and everyone is just being really polite. I obviously need to hang out with more witches. Except, they probably won't want me around because their people wind up dead around me. I can't even blame them.

The drive to the graveside is long and sad. Once there I get out of my car and I walk around a bit while they get set up. Helen is being buried in one of the older sections of the cemetery. It looks like everyone in this section is probably related to her. I didn't even know I was being trained by someone from an old and distinguished line like hers must be to have a whole family section. I realize they are starting and I hurry over to stand at the back of the crowd. One of the women at the front, near the coffin turns and searches me out, walking over when she spots me. I am really nervous about this, because what if they all blame me? She reaches me and says, "I know she was training you, and I just want you to know, you meant a great deal to her. She was very happy and proud to be the one training you."

My mouth gapes and I feel the tears running down my face, "Thank you. That means a lot. I wanted to— I would have done anything— she said I couldn't…"

The lady hugs me, "I know, I know. She told you that you couldn't because she was too close. She knew it was more likely she would take you with her than you be able to bring her back, no matter what power you had. That is an area where science is much more powerful than us. You are one of her close circle, please come stand with us."

"What?"

"You were here student, you belong with us. Not standing back here mourning alone."

I nod and walk with her because if I try to speak all that is going to come out is blubbering. I want to make Helen proud, not exasperated. The service is sweet and relatively short. We watch as her casket is lowered into the earth. As we move away so that others can pay any final respects to her they ask if I will come to the gathering. As they speak a breeze passes through carrying with it the scents of Leonidas and Sebastian. I look and spot them leaning against Sebastian's car, "No. I think I will need to meet with my shadows over there." She follows my gaze, "And remind them that even though I am sad I am a grown person."

The woman chuckles, "Let them shadow you. They care and you are surrounded by danger. It is good for even a fierce one such as you to have her protectors."

"How did you know that?"

"I see the energies around you. Some call it auras, but I think that isn't quite right for me. Because what I see isn't just you, it is other energies affecting you as well."

"Well that is wild. Thank you. I will keep that in mind when I feel a little smothered."

She puts a hand on my arm, "Good. And be safe. We'll be in touch with you soon."

I start to ask about what but she has turned and walked back to the crowd, much faster than I would think possible for her. Shrugging I turn to walk toward the guys. I guess I will find out when she gets in touch with me. The guys look a little guilty as I walk toward them, it makes me laugh a little.

Suddenly Mikael is in front of me and I stop short to avoid walking through him. He crosses his arms and looks down at me, "How many friends will you lose before you admit that I am the only one that can truly keep you safe? How many more funerals? Will you kill them all to avoid me? You used to love me. Now their blood is on your hands. You are nothing but a danger to them."

Oh, he knows how to twist the knife in my heart. "Why are you here Mikael? Is it really blood on my hands if their deaths are your fault? Where do you find all this fucking audacity?"

Before he can reply Leonidas and Sebastian are standing on either side of me. Mikael sneers at them, "Oh look, your little friends have come out to play. Maybe the next one to go will be one of them."

Leonidas laughs, "This from the man hiding behind a witch? The boy that won't face anyone directly since his house got dropped on him?"

Sebastian laughs and Mikael scowls, "What would you know about it? You turned and ran. Both of you."

Leonidas watches him through hooded eyes as he brushes some imaginary dust from his shoulder, "We are here now. Where exactly are you? Care to talk about these things in person?"

Mikael laughs and fades away. Sebastian looks over at Leonidas, "When we find him, he pays for all of it."

Leonidas nods his agreement and I speak up, "Um, hello. I don't want him killed if we can avoid that."

Leonidas smiles, "There are lots of ways to make a vampire pay without killing them."

Sebastian chimes in with, "Exactly. And we would just like the opportunity to explore these ways and see if there are others as well. For science."

I raise a brow at them, "For science? Blood thirsty heathens. Both of you. What are you doing here?" Even as I ask them the question I know they are going to keep doing it if for no other reason than Mikael showed up and they got to intercede.

"We," Sebastian points at himself and Leonidas, "felt like you shouldn't be alone in your time of need. Plus, we were concerned that Mikael might try to catch you alone. Which, I want to point out here, he did."

Leonidas nods, "Exactly. We are here looking after you. It is what lovers do. They take care of each other."

The witch's words ring in my ears. Hanging my head I give in. "Ok. I give. And I appreciate you both caring for me so much that you would follow me out here and hang around the car just to make sure I was safe."

Leonidas grins, "Great. We are forgiven. So, uh, can I ride with you?"

I tilt my head a little, "Why? I mean, you came with Sebastian, right?"

"I did. And I don't like the way this guy drives with me in the car. Plus, you are hella cuter than he is."

Sebastian crosses his arms and raises a brow, "You are a vampire, what the hell are you worried about?"

Leonidas says, "I'm worried about my beautiful face! I don't want you fucking it up to get rid of me and have her all to yourself."

I can't help but laugh when he says that. Sebastian rolls his eyes, "On that note, I am going back to the house. You better hope she gives you a ride."

He starts to head toward his car and I run over to stop him, "Wait. You didn't say good bye." He wraps his arms around me and lifts me up, crushing his lips to mine. My arms slip around his shoulders to twine in his hair as my mouth opens to his. The kiss heats up till I feel certain I might catch fire.

Sebastian breaks the kiss off, sets me down very gently and whispers next to my ear, "If I don't stop now I am taking you right here on one of the graves. I'll see you at the house."

My lips are swollen and I am breathless, I just nod. He takes his hands from my waist, caresses my cheek and starts walking to his car. I walk over to Leonidas and ask, "Ready to go?"

"Oddly enough I am ready to finish what he started. Shit. I didn't think I would be ok seeing that but not only am I ok with it, I am really turned on."

"Well, he did have a point about not fucking on graves. So, let's go to the car."

He laughs and puts an arm around me as we pick our way through graves and head for my car.

Eighteen

Jasmine

It's raining today. I love rainy days. Especially right now as they suit my mood. It has only been a day since we put Helen in the ground. My heart hurts to think of her in the cold ground and I have to remind myself that she isn't there. I want her to still be with us. Tonight I should be at lessons.

I know this will get easier, the pain will be lesser eventually, but I sure would like to skip some of this. I turn away from the window in my bedroom just in time to see Hekate materialize.

"Hello dear one. I am so sorry for your loss."

"Thank you. I am missing her something fierce today when I know my lessons should be tonight."

Hekate nods, "I understand. I have news about your lessons. Would you like to sit?"

"I feel like I should have offered you a place to sit." I wrap my arms around myself, "I don't have any chairs in here though. We can sit on the bed or we can go to one of the areas that has chairs?"

Hekate smiles indulgently at me as she waves her hand and two overstuffed chairs appear behind her. The chairs are angled to face each other and the window. I bow my head to her, "Thank you. Yes."

I walk over and sit down, pulling my feet up under me. She sits in her chair with much more decorum than I have in me right now. "Jasmine, the witches still want to train you."

My eyes open wide, "What? No! They can't risk themselves like that! No! I'll figure it out. It will be fine, I'm sure of it. They are so fragile, I can't. I can't see another one die in my arms."

Hekate sighs, "I understand child. That will never get easier. But, these witches know the score. They don't want you to lack in training and they also want to be safe. They have decided you will have a new teacher every week. They will all communicate with each other and it might be challenging to learn from so many different styles, but this will help to keep anyone from guessing that they are important to you, keeping them safe from those that seek to tear you apart."

"It's Mikael isn't it?"

"Yes. And others."

"Great. So he is still hiring out for my murder. That's nice. I hope that he chokes on their fees. Winds up in the poor house. I just, I hope he suffers the way he is making so many others suffer."

"I know. He will one day. And he will blame you, though it is all the results of his own actions. The witches will contact you. Go to them. Keep learning. Do not let Mikael win by stripping you of all the things you love. They will be on their guard for attacks now and so will you. Now, will you do this thing? Will you continue to learn from the witches community?"

I nod, "I will. I am terrified for each one of them but I will do as you ask."

"Excellent. It is good you are not giving up. We can't let him and others like him think they get to win. I must go now." She stands and walks over to me, "Keep the chairs, consider them a late housewarming gift." She leans down and kisses my forehead. "You are so much more amazing than you give yourself credit for. Rest, recuperate. Your time to fight will come all too soon."

Nineteen

Mikael

Hake has shown up unexpectedly after being off grid for a week. Vigo has gone to escort him in the house. The sky is glorious tonight and my study has a good view. I don't spend enough time enjoying the stars. I have been too caught up in the world of late. So many little details to attend to so the money keeps flowing as it should. And this mess with Jasmine. I still don't understand why things will change so drastically if she doesn't choose me, but I know they will.

Hake enters the room and Vigo closes the door behind him, leaving us alone. "Where have you been Hake?" I ask in a quiet voice.

He shivers, "I have been hiding. I couldn't be sure she didn't see it happen and I had to hide."

I turn from the window to face him, "What do you mean you couldn't be sure she didn't see it happen? See what happen?"

"Her friend from the bookstore. I happened to be walking through a magical section of town and I spotted her friend so I killed her. Then Jasmine came running out and I was terrified that she had seen me. I have been in hiding all week just in case she did. I still managed to throw a shade of you at her, at the funeral no less. There was interference, but nothing major."

"I see. You have been busy."

"I have, I told you I would be working and I intend to fulfill my end of the deal. I want immortality."

"Hmm, yes. A fine thing to crave when you don't have it, I imagine. Very well. You can do your magic from here, correct? You don't need to be in town to reach her?"

"No, I don't have to be anywhere near her to send your shade at her."

"Then you will stay here. I will keep you safe from harm and you will continue to work. Vigo!"

The door opens as his name leaves my mouth. "Yes sir?"

"Our guest will be staying. Give him a room and order food for him. He will need something other that blood and alcohol. Perhaps work with him about what foods he eats. I seem to recall humans being picky about that sort of thing."

Vigo nods with a grimace, "Yes sir. If you would come with me Hake."

Hake follows Vigo out of the room, leaving me to bask in the fact that plans are coming together.

Twenty

Jasmine

The club really did burn to the ground. Some of the asphalt of the parking lot got so hot it melted. I got in contact with the owner of the club today and he said that he won't be reopening but he would be willing to sell the licensing with the property. Meaning that I wouldn't have to wait for a liquor license, it would come with the property.

I brought Chloe and Scarlett out to get their opinions on it. I have this idea of reopening Club Amnesia as a place for the magical community. Still a strip club, but a good one and magical people instead of regular humans. I have learned so much about this area now that I am a vampire. There are a lot of people in the magical community living here. Strip clubs are fun as long as they are run right.

. . .

Chloe and Scarlett stepped away to discuss my idea. I am not sure why but what ever. They'll tell me eventually. Ah, they are walking over now.

Chloe looks very stern, "We have talked this over and we have come to a decision. You may not like it."

I nod and Scarlett picks up where Chloe left off, "But we really feel like this will be for the best. So, we want to be your partners in this venture. Not silent partners either. Obviously, this isn't about whether or not any of us could afford this. We want in because things like this keep vampires living. This could be lucrative, fun, and keep us part of the world. What do you think?"

"Really? You think it is good and you want in?"

Scarlett nods, "Really we do."

"Yes! Hell yes! I can't think of anyone that I would rather work with than you two. Thank you!" I step forward and wrap my arms around the two of them, pulling us all close for a quick group hug. "I will let him know we want it. This is going to be so great! Though the building portion of this is probably going to be a time and money suck. The parking lot too."

"Better we start out with the big investment to be right out of the gate than have to patch it and be bullshit forever." Chloe says as she turns to look at the ashes of the building. "You think Leonidas' company has time to do this or we need to do the research and find someone else?"

Shrugging I say, "Maybe? We'll have to check in with him. I don't know how busy he keeps his crews. I feel like he would open his calendar for us though. Or push his calendar up.

We'll figure it out. Don't worry." No sooner than I say not to worry Mikael appears in front of me. I can tell that they see him to by the shocked expressions on their faces. "The fuck are you doing here Mikael?"

He sneers at me, "What do you think I am doing here? I am checking on my property. What are you doing here? This place was burnt to the ground for a reason. You don't belong in these kinds of places. Go home."

That's it. He found my last straw and stomped on that bitch. I am so fucking done with his shit. I pull up the spell that I saw Helen use on the other shade and I throw it at Mikael as I say, "I'll be seeing you real fucking soon asshole." The aggravation was almost worth the look on his face just then.

Mikael

I watch as Jasmine throws something at the shade of me, then the vision goes black and Hake flies across the room to hit the wall. Vigo picks him up and places him on a couch. How did she do that? And what did she mean when she said she would see us real soon? She can't know where I am. She hasn't got the resources to find me.

Hake is coming round, could he know something about this? As Hake's eyes start to open he suddenly sits up straight, "How is she powerful enough to do this? She shouldn't be able to do that and she did. She wasn't even drained a little after throwing that at us. She threw me across the room without even knowing my physical location!"

"Pfft," crossing my arms I say, "She is not that strong. This is a fluke. She has tried to kill me twice and here I am. If she were that strong I would be dead by now. All she has going for her is dumb luck. She hasn't even got the training to make use of what she does have."

Hake shakes his head no, "You don't understand what she just did. I begin to think you don't understand magic at all. You have seriously underestimated her abilities and in doing so you may have signed both our death warrants."

One eyebrow raised I say, "Maybe you just aren't as powerful or talented as you thought you were."

Twenty-One

Jasmine

I make it home in record time. I know where that bastard is and I am so done playing nice. Pulling into the driveway I slam the car into park. Turning it off and snatching the keys I run in the house to change my clothes. I want to be able to move when I face that asshole. I grab a piece of paper and leave a note telling everyone where I am going. Sort of. I don't have an actual address. But I can see how to get there in my head.

Dropping the note on my bed I walk out heading for the front door. Opening it I see everyone lined up on the porch. Chloe, Scarlett, Leonidas, Sebastian, and Eason. "Um. What are you all doing here… right now…"

Leonidas steps forward, "Stopping you from going off and getting killed without us. You can't leave us behind. We are going with you or you aren't going. Period."

I look at each of them, they look so determined. I have to try at least. "You can't go. He won't attack me from the start if I go in alone. I could get him alone and kill him before he realized what was happening. And you would all stay safe. I need you all to be safe."

Leonidas reaches out and puts his hands on my shoulders, waiting until I look at him, "Jasmine, we need the same from you. You can't know that he won't immediately attack you. What if he managed to cage you somehow? He may be waiting for you to rush up there. We are all of us stronger together. Let's do this together. We all agree with you, we need to put a stop to him. But together."

"I don't like it. But you all are right. And I would hate it if you did this to me."

"Good. So none of us will do this to anyone else. We fight side by side or not at all."

Twenty-Two

Jasmine

My stomach churns at the idea of putting everyone in danger like this. I guess I don't have much choice though. I couldn't think of a single good argument that wasn't selfish in some way. We decided to think things through so now we have moved to the kitchen. Someone found a map and they want me to figure out a way to get what is in my head onto the map.

We spread it out on the table and I close my eyes for a moment, focusing on getting the point in my head to be visible to me in the correct place on the map. Opening my eyes I look down and I can see a light marking where we are now with a line of light leading from that to another place to the north west of the city. A pencil is shoved into my hand, I trace the light from one place on the map to the other. Word appear in my mind's eye so I write them down too. Closing my eyes I release the need to see it that way while holding the thread of the tag. I won't be letting go of that until I find them.

"Purgatory Lane?" Eason says, "He lives on Purgatory Lane? Wow. That is creepy sounding."

Sebastian nods in agreement, "I think I might pick a different place but, that's just me." He moves his gaze from the map to grin at me, "Looks like we are heading to purgatory."

Scarlett rolls her eyes, "I want to point out that dickface obviously has some way of tracking her, of knowing where she is. It is very likely the makers bond, but we can't be sure. If you head up there with all of us Jasmine, there is no chance of being sneaky. It gives him that advantage. As much as I know you will hate this idea, I think we need to split up."

Leonidas, one arm folded across his chest and the other resting on it and rubbing his chin, "She's right. If we send a crew up there without you first, they would be able to get around the place, scout it and have some idea of what we face. As long as you, Jasmine, stay well the fuck away from there for long enough to do the recon and make a plan after."

Sebastian folds his arms across his chest, "I like it. But someone will need to stay and help Jasmine stay in town doing things. In case they are monitoring her movements."

Scarlett laughs, "Unfortunately, I have a lot of experience creeping about spying on people so I can't volunteer for staying with you or I would. But I am better suited to being out there. I'll be out there, which of you boys will be staying with her?"

"I am right here. You see me don't you?"

Sebastian blushes as he says, "I um, I have some training I don't want to discuss that actually makes me more suited to being out there. I would much rather be helping Jasmine, but I've been a sneaky bastard for a long time."

Leonidas bites his lip and grins, "Guess I am the lucky winner that gets to stay with you. I am a lot more of a tear it all down and ask questions later kind of guy."

Sebastian chuckles, "Ok then. I actually brought my suburban. Let's all load up in that, those of us that are going first, and we should make it there not long after the sun sets."

I hug everyone on the way out, telling them all to be careful and whispering incantations over them to make peoples eyes slide away from them. It is the best I can do for mow. Maybe once I find the library door I can learn some better spells.

We wait another ten minutes after they leave to wander out to the hardware store.

Leonidas

The hardware store is large and perfect for what I need to do. We get in there and I tell Jasmine, "Hey, while you pick out chains I am going over a few aisles and grab some things. I'll be right back."

I leave her staring at my back like I've grown a second head. Which is fine as long as she doesn't follow me. As soon as I make it a few aisles away I duck down one and keep walking, zig-zagging my way to the far back corner of the store while I call Ben. As soon as he answers I tell him to hold on and I call Banner, connecting the two calls. Banner answers and I quickly explain what is going on, "Now I need both of you to gather up whoever is willing to fight and head to the address Scarlett gives you. We are finally going to get that bastard Mikael and I want to make sure we do it right. I have to go. I'm sending you both Scarlett's contact information. We clear?"

They both say they are and I end the call. I grab some netting from the aisle I am in, good sturdy stuff that we don't need at all, and send out Scarlett's contact info as I start walking back to where I left Jasmine. I send one more message, this one to Scarlett, letting her know what I did. She sends back a laugh emoji. Oh man. I hope Jasmine doesn't hate me for this.

I get back to Jasmine and she has grabbed two lengths of chain. She is eyeing a digging rod when I reach her. She drops the chains in my arms and pick it up, giving it a few slow swings. She nods and takes the chains back, "You ready to check out?"

"Yes. What is the digging rod for?"

"Digging rod? Oh! Well, it just looks like a really good skull basher. If I have to fight I mean to take a motherfucker out. The days of me getting beaten are long gone and I'm not letting them come back."

I nod and decide I am leaving all of that alone. We check out and I pay because I want her to know I fully support her knocking heads, even if I prefer the heads not be mine. We get to the car and it just hasn't been long enough. Looking across the roof of the car at her I say, "You know, I am thinking that maybe you should hunt before you go up there? You know, fresh blood and peak strength, all that."

She scowls at me, "I don't like it. You're probably right but I still don't damn like it. I want to go make him stop. But fine. We'll go hunting."

"Great. I love watching you take lives. Your savagery turns me on something fierce."

She laughs, "Pervert! Get in the car."

She drives us over to the downtown area. Getting out she says, "Get away from me while I hunt. Not that I worry about attacking you, I don't want you scaring away my food."

I laugh out loud at that, "Yes ma'am." She takes off down an alley while I walk around the building along the main route. I spot my mark pretty quickly. He is following some young girls. The girls are afraid, I can smell the stench of it. I walk a little faster till I come even with him and fall into step with him. "Nice night for hunting isn't it?"

He smiles over at me, "Indeed it is friend. Haven't seen you hunting these parts. Where you from?"

"Oh, I am on my way to a club made for hunters. You should come, it's very exclusive, invite only."

He looks so excited by the prospect I want to kill him where he stands. He agrees and I lead him down an alley, telling him the door is toward the end. We get past the dumpsters, he sees no door and starts to panic. That's when I lift him up and slam him against the wall, "Where are you going friend? The party is just starting." He starts to scream until I bite him. His warm blood fills my mouth and I drink greedily. He moans instead and I bite harder. I don't want this fucker to enjoy any of it. I want him to die in pain.

He gets close to death and I pull away.licking his neck so it heals. I watch for it to finish healing and as soon as it does I snatch his head around, breaking his neck. A few more hits and into the dumpster with him. Now, to find Jasmine. Back out of the alley I scent the air. She isn't far. I follow her scent and I arrive just in time to see her leading a really big guy down the alley before me. I follow quietly, keeping to the shadows. The guy is telling her how he likes his women submissive and if they aren't he just makes them submit anyway. She chuckles at his words and I lean against a wall to watch the show as she stops and turns to face him. I watch him leer down at her, "Get on your knees bitch."

She laughs at him and kicks his right foot out from under him. He hits the ground and she grabs his shirt to pull him up before his head stops bouncing. His head lolls to one side as she pulls him close and sinks her teeth into his neck. He moans in pleasure as she drinks before he realizes he is dying. His struggles are weak and her hold on him is firm. He drags an arm up, but loses strength before grasping her arm and his hand falls to hang limply. She releases his throat but spits on him to heal him. She drops him back to the pavement. Stepping to one side she hefts him and tosses him in the corner next to the dumpster. Turning to face me she says, "Now can we go?"

Twenty-Three

Scarlett

We are parking down the road from the place when my phone rings. I have no idea who it is but I have a feeling I should answer it so I do, "Hello?"

"Hi, is this Scarlett? My name is Ben. I am part of Leonidas's clan. He asked that we call you to coordinate coming to help."

"Oh! Wonderful. Yes, wait, I have another call coming in…"

"That is probably Banner. One of the wolves that works for Leonidas."

"Ok. Hold on while I connect the calls."

I sort out the calls so that we can all talk, "How long will it take you to get to the northwest side of town and how many will you have with you?"

Ben says, "I'll have five. Possibly more. And maybe ten minutes."

Banner chuckles, "I have ten. All of them wolves. We are five minutes away and getting closer."

"I am sending you my location. Come here and park next to the suburban. Wait till we get back from scouting and we'll go from there."

Sebastian and myself have the most experience sneaking around so it is decided that we will do the recon. We split up, he moving toward the back while I scope the front of the place. I see a camera pointed at the road, and another near the parking area. If we want to send her in to be the only thing he sees he couldn't have made it easier for us.

The cameras are it. He has no guards. No tripwires. No motion detectors. Nothing beyond the two cameras. At least from what I can find at least. I meet up with Sebastian on the far side of the house. I give him a rundown of what I found as he tells me there is nothing out back. At all. We head back, each checking the other's assessment. He is correct. There isn't even a flood light out here. This is wild. I mean, if Jasmine had any idea how many cameras I have around the outside of the house she would either be impressed or horrified. I'm not sure which one so I haven't told her about them just yet. I will. One day. Probably. Most likely when she finds them.

Sebastian and I meet up again and stroll through the woods. This place is the height of arrogance and I'm not even surprised. Mikael has always seen himself as invincible. Why would that change just because Jasmine has almost killed him twice now and she still wants to keep him alive? His audacity is mind-boggling. Sebastian is disturbed by the lack of security.

"I can't decide if he is just recklessly over confident in his own abilities or if he is just oblivious. I don't think it very likely he has enough fire power to just be unconcerned."

I chuckle, "Possibly a combination of the two."

Two more vehicles have pulled up while we were scouting. A battered van I recognize as Banner's and a Ram pickup. Everyone is still sitting quietly in the vehicles. Which is good I suppose but doesn't bode well for the teamwork we will need in a few minutes.

We stop in front of the three vehicles and wave at everyone to get out and come over. As they all get out I watch how they walk. The people I am with, I know their strengths and weaknesses. These people I have to guess. The wolves, I like. They walk softly and don't make much noise as they get out. Little more concerned about the vampires, how are they so loud?

I glance at Sebastian to see him making the same assessments. His raised brows as he cuts his eyes at me tell me he noticed the same thing about the vampires. I ask, "Are you thinking what I'm thinking?"

"Vampires to the front with Chloe and Eason, waiting for Jasmine to get through before following her in and wolves at the back with us?"

"Yes. Exactly." We give everyone their directions, visually making sure that all the volumes on all the phones are off completely. We tell them messaging only and not even to use vibrate as a ringer right now. We still have to shut some of the vampire's vibrate options off on their phones. It would appear that they didn't know how to do it. We need to have a talk with Leonidas about his guys.

The wolves are better. They had their phones silenced and vibrate turned off before they got here. Banner clears his throat, "I have a question."

"Go ahead."

"Think you all can be all right with us going in as wolves?"

I grin, "Do you understand hand signals?"

He growls at me, "What kind of hand signals?"

"The usual kind used when sneaking about trying to maintain silence?" My grin grows, "Did you think I was going to ask you to sit or something?"

His eyes narrow, "We understand the former, if you try the latter we will bite you."

I laugh, "Fair enough. Let's get into place."

Sebastian

Scarlett is one of the better people I have partnered with in all my time. The wolves, I could only wish to work with them any time I need to do things like this. After we got into place we set them to patrolling. They seem happy for it and it gives us the chance to get more intel. Scarlett is texting with

Leonidas, she says they are on the way. Leonidas made her feed before she came up here even so she would be at full strength, physically and magically.

Scarlett looks up as the sound of tires on gravel reach us, "It's showtime."

Twenty-Four

Jasmine

I arrive at the house that has been lit up like a beacon for me ever since I sent that shade back. The drive is not terribly long but it isn't short either. I drive up it slow. Leonidas has been in contact with Scarlett and she told him about the cameras. I want to make sure the fuckers see me. Or at least that is what I think I want to happen until a giant sinkhole opens up in the middle of the driveway. I look to Leonidas, "I'll keep them focused on me. You go around through the trees and catch up when you can."

He touches my shoulder as I turn to open the car door. I look back at him and he puts a hand on either side of my face, drawing me close for a kiss. He kisses me softly and whispers against my lips, "Make sure you come back to me."

"I will." I get out of the car and walk up to the edge of the sink hole. As I call the wind to float me over the sink hole I just hope I can keep my promise.

Mikael

We are watching as she arrives. When Hake opens the sink hole I am sure she will cry. Instead the bitch floats over it. I told her not to use her magic! I look to Vigo, "Send everyone at her!"

Vigo click the button on the walkie, "Everyone after the bitch! Cut her down!"

Answers come through, one is cut off even as he tries to speak. Banging the table with my fist I yell, "The bitch has backup! Tell them to kill that bitch! And you!" I point over at Hake, "Make yourself useful!"

Jasmine

I touch down on the far side and Leonidas is there telling me, "Fuck that noise. If you go I'm going with you."

I laugh, "Guess I'll have to make sure I don't die just so you'll be able to stick around. Tell everyone to stay away from Mikael. He is mine. I don't know what I am going to do about him yet, but I don't want him to have the opportunity to hurt anyone else."

He nods and fires off a text as a bunch of guys pour out of the house in front of us and some more come out of the woods next to us led by Chloe and Eason. A couple wolves come out from the other side and they are fucking huge. These have to be shifters, which means they are probably Leonidas's crew. Fuck yes! They run in and take out a couple guys before anyone else sees them and we hear screams of "Kill the bitch" coming over the radios. Guess that's our cue.

Twenty-Five

Jasmine

I do believe I am the bitch everyone is speaking of as they are
all now rushing at me. Fuck. What would Hekate do? Not
fire, fur burns. Ice! I get off a few shots when a wolf howls
and I hear more answer from around back as a lot more men
rush out of the house. I don't think these are humans either.
At least, not all of them. I start sending shield shaped blasts
of ice into the crowd trying to get at me and I am making
some headway when I feel a power building in the air.

Fuck me, what the hell is this? Shit. Shit. Shit. I have to
protect them, but how? House shield! Yes! I throw it up and
cut a few people in half or less. There are definitely some
body parts laying around now that are still real fresh. But I
got everyone that is here for me shielded and that is what
counts as I watch lightening rain down from the sky. Some of
their people are hit by it but I can't see much more than that
as two guys make it past everyone to advance on me. The

shield is taking strength I don't have to hold it as the men outside it batter away trying to get inside. I want to open a hole under them but I don't know if I could keep it that small. I hope they are just human as they are in reach now and I swing on one hoping to knock him into the other. It doesn't work exactly like I hoped. I knocked one the fuck out but the other side stepped and grabbed me. I twist in his arms and wrap mine around him, "And Leonidas was worried I would need to be fed before I got here," I say with terrible smile as I sink my teeth into his chest and start to drink. The guy grabs my hair, trying to pull me off but I drain him and drop him only when he stops fighting. I lean down, clasping his head with both hands and twisting sharp till I hear the bones snap. The shield around us fails, I can't hold it against so many. I send ice shields flying through the crowds again. They shatter as they mow people down and some of the shards find homes in the bellies of my attackers.

I call winds in and start flinging men as far as I can, I am never going to be able to listen to the song It's Raining Men the same way again. I'm just going to see this from now on. Another man makes it to me, diving into me and knocking me to the ground. Didn't save his comrade who ended up hitting the trunk of a nearby tree.

We roll and I am trying to get a hold on him when he is ripped off of me and his throat torn out, blood spraying all over me before Leonidas throws him at some other attackers. He helps me up and asks, "Are you all right?"

I nod, just in awe of his viciousness. He turns and meets another one head on. I start picking people up with magic and throwing them at the house one after the other. How did he have so many fuckers here hiding? I start aiming for the windows, but my aim is shit so there are still a lot of horrible bone breaking wet splats happening as these fuckers hit the walls. I hope Mikael is terrified listening to this.

I feel the magic start to build and I decide to try something else. I take the house spell and make tiny ones to go around each person on our side. It's a hell of a drain on my energy, but there is fresh meat everywhere. The magic is at a fever pitch when I grab a guy and start drinking. Oh, and he's a vampire, even better. His blood washes away the exhaustion creeping at the edges, giving me new life even as I take his. The ground opens underneath us. As we fall I frantically use the shields around each of them to snatch them and myself into the air and toward the house. I drop us all none too gently on the other side of the hole that is closing over pretty well everyone we were fighting that hasn't been flung elsewhere.

Did not see that coming. Going to bet they thought it would work out different too. Sebastian comes over dragging a body. "Here, feed. You're burning through too fast. This one is still alive."

I rasp out, "Thank you," just before I bite into this one's neck. The hot blood is human this time and he would have died soon either way. Refreshed I let Sebastian help me up and I ask, "Is anyone hurt? Did we lose anyone?" Banner is suddenly standing before me naked and covered in blood as he tells me, "We lost a wolf and a vampire to the enemy."

"Dammit. He is going to pay for their deaths too. Let's go." Banner shifts, he and another wolf flank me as we head for the door.

Twenty-Six

Jasmine

Of course there are more new vampires in here. Where the fuck did he find all of them? Is there a job board or something? New vampire seeks short term employment to take care of this pesky immortality problem? My people rush in and start taking motherfuckers out. I need to find Mikael. That is the only way to stop this. And his fucking witch. The wolves leave my side almost immediately as they keep other assholes off me.

I see Mikael enter the giant hall we are fighting in and start towards me. I am going to shock the hell out of him. Once he appears dead the rest of these assholes will surely be done with us because they won't be getting paid anymore. Leonidas steps in front of me as he drains a guy then tosses his limp body at Mikael's feet.

I reach up and touch his shoulder, "Mikael is mine love."

He growls but then what I said reaches him and he steps aside as he takes my bloody hand in his, raising it to his lips for a kiss.

Mikael laughs as he steps over the body, "I always knew you were the kind of bitch to let a woman do the fighting for you Leonidas."

Leonidas narrows his eyes at him but takes off to the side after some skinny guy with a knife. He grabs the man's arm and forces him to plant the dagger into the floor. Mikael tries to take advantage of my seeming distraction and leap at me, I send up a blast of air to knock him away. I feel magic building again and I focus to pinpoint where it is going. Once I lock onto the area I send bolts of lightening through walls in that direction. The pressure of the magic building disappears and Mikael tackles me to the ground. I open my eyes and see Leonidas rip the skinny man's head clean off his shoulders as I send a blast of magic out from my core, sending Mikael flying at the far wall with only a little of my skin going with him. I get to my feet as he is hitting the ground and getting to his feet.

He taunts me as he dusts himself, "Why not try fighting me without the magic you stole from me? Could it be because you know you are nothing without it? That you could never best me without it and even with it you struggle?"

I laugh at him, "Really Mikael? Gaslighting? That's the best you have? The magic was always intended for me. You were just a vessel for delivery." I tell him as I build a fireball. As he starts to scream about my lies I launch it at him. He goes up like a well laid fireplace. He tries to run but I wrap him in a band of air to stop him. I let the tears flow as he screams. "I never wanted this Mikael. I'm so sorry. I'm so damn sorry it had to be this way Mikael." I fall to my knees as his screams stop and he turns to ash. Two of the wolves come to sit next to me, pressing their warm bodies against me as I cry.

Then Leonidas is there, lifting me up and holding me close as I cry out my heartbreak over Mikael leaving me no other choice.

Twenty-Seven

Jasmine

Once I manage to get myself together, with the help of my people, we decide to search the house. We need to know if I got that witch that was casting against us or if we need to watch our backs in the future. I keep magic at the ready as we walk through, which means my hands are glowing with power and we turn on lights just to be thorough.

Walking into the farthest room that still got hit by lightening we find a mirror with my hair tied around the edges. "This is sick. But also probably how he has been watching me all this time." I set it on fire and make sure it burns into dust. We check all around the mirror and the counters and such in this room but whoever was here isn't anymore and they don't seem to have left a forwarding address either. Dammit. We search the rest of the house to no avail. We do find some guys that lived and decided to sit things out after I threw them through windows. Nice to know I did hit the mark with some of them. They ask to join us and Leonidas tells them that they will need to prove themselves to Ben. They nod and wander off downstairs after telling us that no one came through to hide with them.

When we quit finding bodies we know that the witch has well and truly escaped. This is no good. No damn good. The only reason to run is if you think you are going to be killed or you still want to get your revenge. I guess now I have some unknown fucking witch out there just dying to kill me because Mikael is a complete and utter ballsack. We head back downstairs and Scarlett looks at me, "Hey Jasmine, we dragged all the bodies in the house. Think you could make it burn to the ground before the fire department gets here?"

I smile, "I think I could actually."

Twenty-Eight

Jasmine

It's been two days since I burnt Mikael to the ground. I still feel bad for doing it. I haven't really been alone since then. If Scarlett isn't nearby then Sebastian or Leonidas are. I think they are worried about me. I have spent the better part of two days in bed.

Today is the day I drag myself out though. If only to figure out what they are banging on out there. I get up and wander out. Moving my nightgown into place so my tits aren't hanging out. Tank tops. So comfy but so not willing to stay in place. I find Scarlett and Sebastian in the living area reading. It must be Leonidas. I walk around listening to the banging. I see Leonidas in the kitchen as I pass by hunting the sound. Coming to an intersection of hallways I stop and turn my head to the right following the sound to see a door at the far end of the hallway. A door that shouldn't exist. That is where the banging is coming from. I bring my phone up and hit the priest's name in my contacts.

"Father Neally? I think we have a problem."

"Oh? What's that my dear?"

"Well, I haven't been able to find the door since Caden brought The whole crew over and Lacey was rude as fuck. Tonight though, tonight the door is visible and something is banging on it from the other side."

"Oh no! This is not good. Not good. I'll be right there!"

I look at my phone, I think he just hung up on me. Shit.

Rhiannon writes steamy paranormal romance. She is an avid reader of many authors in a variety of genre though she tends more toward paranormal.

She has three former pound puppies that she dotes on and three daughters that she adores.

Rhiannon has lived in multiple states though she is currently residing in North Carolina. Wandering, witching, and reading with her puppies and husband are what she does when she isn't writing.

To learn about what is happening in Rhiannon's world and get loads of pupper cuteness, sign up for the by using the QR code below to visit my website.

Pursuit of the Vampire King

Prey of the Vampire King

Reign of the Vampire King

Coming Soon

Love and Vampires Series

Olivia's Fall

Olivia's Prison

Olivia's Flight

Olivia's Family

Warriors of the Old Gods

A Dream of Blood

A Dream of Wolves

A Dream of Stone

A Dream of Ravens

A Dream of Bones